Ford Madox Ford

The Brown Owl

A Fairy Story. Vol. I

Ford Madox Ford

The Brown Owl
A Fairy Story. Vol. I

ISBN/EAN: 9783744748797

Printed in Europe, USA, Canada, Australia, Japan

Cover: Foto ©Andreas Hilbeck / pixelio.de

More available books at **www.hansebooks.com**

THE CHILDREN'S LIBRARY

VOLUME ONE

THE BROWN OWL

THE CHILDREN'S LIBRARY.

THE
BROWN OWL

A Fairy Story

BY

FORD H. MADOX HUEFFER

TWO ILLUSTRATIONS BY
F. MADOX BROWN

NEW YORK
CASSELL PUBLISHING COMPANY
104 & 106 FOURTH AVENUE
1892

THIRD EDITION

THE BROWN OWL

ONCE upon a time, a long while ago—in fact long before Egypt had risen to power and before Rome or Greece had ever been heard of—and that was some time before you were born, you know—there was a king who reigned over a very large and powerful kingdom.

Now this king was rather old, he had founded his kingdom himself, and he had reigned over it nine hundred and ninety-nine and a half years already. As I have said before, it was a very large kingdom, for it contained, among other things, the whole of the western half of the world. The rest of

the world was divided into smaller
kingdoms, and each kingdom was ruled
over by separate princes, who, however,
were none of them so old as Intafernes, as he was called.

Now King Intafernes was an ex-
ceedingly powerful magician — that
was why he had remained so long
on the throne; for you must know that
in this country the people were divided
into two classes—those who were magicians, and those who weren't.   The
magicians called themselves Aristocrats,
and the others called themselves what
they liked; also in this country, as in
all other countries, the rich magicians
had the upper hand over the rest, but
still the others did not grumble, for
they were not badly treated on the
whole.   Now of all the magicians in
the country the King was the greatest,
and no one approached him in magic
power but the Chancellor, who was
called Merrymineral, and he even was
no match for the King.

Among other things King Intafernes had a daughter, who was ex-
ceedingly beautiful—as indeed all princesses are or ought to be.   She had a
very fair face, and a wealth of golden
hair that fell over her shoulders, like a
shining waterfall falling in ripples to
her waist.

Now in the thousandth year of her
father's reign the Princess was eighteen,
and in that country she was already of
age.   Three days before her nineteenth
birthday, however, her father fell sick
and gradually weakened, until at last
he had only strength left to lie in his
royal bed.   Still, however, he retained
his faculties, and on the Princess's
birthday he made all the magicians
file before his bed and swear to be
faithful for ever to the Princess.   Last
of all came the Chancellor, the pious
Merrymineral, and as he took the oath
the King looked at him with a loving
glance and said :

'Ah ! my dear Merrymineral, in

truth there was no need for thee to have taken the oath, for it is thy nature to be faithful; and it being thy nature, thou couldst not but be faithful.'

To which the pious Merrymineral answered:

'To such a master and to such a mistress how could I but be faithful?' and to this noble sentiment the three hundred and forty-seven magicians could not help according unanimous applause.

When they were quiet again the King said:

'So be it, good Merrymineral, do thou always act up to thy words. But now leave, good men all, for I am near my end, and would fain spend my last moments with my daughter here.'

Sorrowfully, one by one, the courtiers left, wishing him their last adieux. He had been a good king to all, all through his long reign, and they were sorry that he had to leave them at last.

Soon they were all gone except the good Merrymineral, and at last he too went, his whole frame shaking with suppressed sobs; his body seemed powerless with grief, and his limbs seemed to refuse their functions. The King looked after him, carefully noticing whether the door was shut. Then he spoke :

'My dear daughter,' he said, 'when I am gone be kind to every one, and, above all, cherish the Owl—do cherish the Owl—promise me to cherish the Owl.'

'But how can I cherish the Owl?' cried the poor Princess; 'how can I, unless I know who he is?'

But the King only answered:

'Dear Ismara, do promise to cherish the Owl!'

And he said nothing else for a long time, until at last the Princess saw that the only way to let him rest in peace was to promise, and she said :

'I promise, dear father, but still I

do wish I knew who or what the Owl is that I am to cherish.'

'You will see that in good time,' answered the King. 'Now, my dear Ismara, I shall die happy, and you will be safe. If you had not promised—however, we will let that rest unsaid. Now wheel the bed to where I can see out of the window.'

The Princess did as she was told. Now from this you must not imagine that she was a very strong princess—for she was no stronger than most princesses of her age; but the old King, who was a very powerful magician, as I have told you already, made the bed easy for her to move. He might have made it move of its own accord, but he knew that it would please his daughter to be of service to him, and so he let her move it.

The view from the window was very fine. A dark wood grew in the foreground, and far away over the tree-tops were the blue hills, behind which the

sun was just preparing to retire. And
it seemed angry, the sun, for its face
was dark and clouded, and its beams
smote fiercely on everything, and gilded
the tops of the autumn trees with a
purer gold than their natural tint.
But overhead the clouds spread darkly,
and they reached in a black pall to
the verge of the horizon, forming a black
frame to the red-gold sunset; for only
the extreme west was bright with the
waning light.

The Princess sat on the bed beside
the King, and the dying sun lit them
both and fell with a ruddy glare on
the King's hard countenance, as if it
knew that his work on earth for the
day, and for ever, was done.

'Is it not grand?' cried the old
King, as if the glorious sight warmed
his blood again and made him once
more young. 'And is it not grand to
think of the power that thou hast, my
daughter? If thou but raise thy little
finger armies will move from world's

end to world's end.   Fleets come daily from every land for thee alone; all that thou seest is thine, and utterly within thy power.   Think of the power, the grand power, of swaying the world.'

But long before he had got thus far, the Princess was weeping bitterly— partly at the overwhelming prospect, and partly from her great grief.   She seized her father's hand and kissed it passionately.

'My father, my father,' she cried, 'say not so; they are all thine, not mine, for thou livest still, and all is yet well.'

But the old King cut her short:

'Dost thou see the sun?   Look, its lower rim is already cut by the mountains.   When its disc is hidden I too shall have joined the majority, and my soul will have left my body, and the power will be thine.   But above all cherish the Owl.   Never go out of its sight, for if thou do, some harm will happen.'

As he stopped speaking a flash of

lightning lit up the sky, and the sullen roar of distant thunder followed.

From every church in the land the passing bell tolled forth and the solemn sounds came swelling on the breeze. Again came the flash of lightning, and again the thunder, and now the splash of falling rain accompanied and almost drowned the thunder. The sun's rim was now almost down.

For the last time the old King kissed his daughter, as she hung weeping on his neck. Again the lightning came, but this time the thunder was drowned in a more fearful sound. Never before had the sound been heard, except at the death of the Princess's mother. It was the passing bell of the cathedral of the town. And as its sound went forth throughout the whole land men shook their heads in sorrow, for they knew that the soul of the good King had left his body. Through the whole land the news was known—to every one except to the Princess.

For she lay on the bed passionately
kissing the dead face—not yet cold in
death—and calling on his name in
vain; for the ears of the dead are
closed 'to the voice of the charmer,
charm he never so wisely.'

Gradually the voice of the Princess
died away into low sobs and her breath-
ing came more regularly, and in spite
of the tolling of the death-bell she
slept, worn out by her grief. No one
came near her, for at the Court no
one was allowed to enter the royal
presence without a command, whatever happened. So for a time the
Princess slept on, clasping the still
face to her warm cheek. But at last
the death-cold of the face wakened
her once more to the death-cold of
the world. For a time her wakening
dreams refused to let her believe the
worst, but the stern reality forced
itself on her. She raised herself on
her two arms and gazed through the
darkness at the white face that made

her shudder when her longing eyes
at last traced out its lines as a flash
of lightning lit it up. She sprang off
the bed with a wild impulse of calling
for help.

But no sooner had she got to the
door and had given the call than she
once more fainted and seemed for a
time lifeless.

When she came to herself again she
was in bed in her own room. It was
still night, and at the side of her bed
a night-light was burning in a glass
shade. She could not understand
what it all meant; but her head did
ache so, and she could not tell why
they were making such a noise at the
far end of the room. For you see she
was lying on her back low down in the
pillows, and so she could not see
beyond the foot of the bed. However, she raised herself on her elbow
and looked. For a short time she
could see nothing, for the room was
somewhat dark, as the night-light gave

but little light. But at the other end of the room a large fire was burning, and by its light the Princess saw a strange scene.

For in the middle of the floor she could make out a group of three ladies-in-waiting, who were struggling with a large black object—what it was the Princess could not see, but it seemed to be attempting to attack the Court doctor, who was huddled up in a corner with his umbrella spread out before him, and he was gradually sinking down behind it, giving vent to the most horrible groans and shrieks for mercy, and calling to the ladies to keep it off. However, in spite of their efforts, the 'thing' was gradually drawing them nearer and nearer to the poor doctor.

But the strangest thing of all was that the doctor's face was lit up by two distinct rounds of light. It was just as if some one had turned the light of a bull's-eye lantern on him,

and this the Princess could not understand at all. However, she lay still
and watched.

The doctor got farther and farther
behind the umbrella until only his
head appeared over the top of it. At
last he shrieked :

' Send for a regiment of Lifeguards—
let them shoot the Owl—it is necessary
for the health of the Princess. Owls
are very bad things to have in bed-
rooms—they bring scarlatina, and they
always carry the influenza epidemic.
Lifeguards, I tell you, send for them.'
But still the ' thing ' came nearer, and
with an agonised shriek of ' The Owl !'
he sank altogether under the rim.

This loud cry of ' The Owl ' roused
the Princess, and she remembered her
promise to cherish the Owl. So she
called to the ladies-in-waiting, and they,
astonished, let go the thing, and the
Owl immediately flew at the umbrella,
underneath which the doctor was
coiled up, and perched on the top.

The Princess, however, thought it was rather rash to have promised to cherish the Owl if it was going to eat up her physicians in that reckless manner. However, the Owl did not seem aggressive, and only seemed as if it were waiting for further orders. The Princess determined to see if it would come when it was called, like a dog. So she called in a sweet, persuasive voice :

'Come here, good Owl.'

Immediately the dark shape of the Owl flitted noiselessly to her side as she sat on the bed. The wind of its flight blew out the flickering night-light in spite of the glass shade. But the glittering eyes of the Owl lit up the whole room, so that there was no need of light. As it alighted on the bed it turned its eyes on the Princess as much as to say, 'What shall I do now ? '

But the fierce light of the eyes was softened as it turned to her, as if the

Owl feared to hurt her with the blind-
ing rays.

'Cherished Owl,' said the Princess,
'why didst thou hurt the physician?'

The Owl shook his head; but the
Princess could not understand whether
he meant that he did not know why
he had hurt him, or if he meant he
had not hurt him. So the Princess
told one of the ladies-in-waiting to
remove the umbrella from over the
doctor. But this was not so easy as
it sounded, for the doctor held firmly
on to the handle, and in spite of the
united efforts of the three ladies-in-
waiting he managed to hold on. At
last the Princess lost patience.

'Go and help them, good Owl,' she
said; and the Owl, overjoyed, flew to
the doctor, and seizing the top of the
umbrella flew with it up to the ceiling,
and as the doctor still held on, he
flew round and round, until the doctor,
hitting the top of a cupboard, let go,
and fell in a heap in the middle of

the floor, where he lay half unconscious, repeating as he sat:

'Orange juice for influenza; try a seidlitz powder and a blue pill, and keep the owls out of the room and take a warm bath, and—send for the Lifeguards.'

But the Princess did not seem inclined to send for them; and in truth it would have been rather awkward for the horses to get in, as the room was on the second floor.

So the Princess told the ladies-in-waiting to drag him out of the room, and they obeyed; but as he went he said: 'Sleeping in unaired sheets causes rheumatism, sciatica, pleurisy, pneumonia and—owls;' and as the door closed they heard him say, 'Gregory powder and Epsom salts.'

The poor Princess, however, began to weep again, and the Owl sat perched on the bed-post at her feet, watching her with his bright eyes.

However, after she had cried thus

for a long time, she thought it would be better to stop her tears, for they were all in vain, as she knew but too well.

So she rose from her bed; for you must know she had only been laid on her bed when she had fainted, and so she still had all her clothes on.

Through the window - blinds the light of dawn was already beginning to show itself. So the Princess went to the window and drew back the curtains, and let the bright sunlight shine into the room. A beautiful day was dawning after the last night's rain, and the sun was rising brightly over the edge of the blue sea. For a moment, as she looked out, everything was quiet except the shrill chirp of a solitary sparrow that seemed to have awakened too early. From the chimneys of the red-roofed town below her no smoke was rising, for all in the town were asleep still.

Suddenly, with a rush, the morning

breeze came from over the land behind
her, and with the rustle of the wind
everything seemed to wake and come
to life once more. The solitary chirp
of the sparrow was drowned in the
flood of song that poured forth from
the trees in the palace garden, and
with the birds the rest of the living
animals awoke, and from far inland
the lowing of the cows was borne on
the breeze, and now and again came
the joyful bark of the shepherd's dog
as it recognised its master's whistle as
he called it to work again among the
sheep, whose plaintive bleating came
softly, as if from a distance, to the
Princess's ear.

Everything seemed joyful at the
sight of the beautiful morning except
the Princess, and she felt oh so lonely,
for it seemed as if her only friend had
gone from her for ever. And at the
thought her tears began to flow afresh,
for she felt very lonely, while everything else seemed to rejoice. But as

she leant thus against the window-sill, with a great lump in her throat and the hot tears in her eyes, she suddenly felt a weight on her shoulder and a rushing wind waved her hair, and as she turned her head to see what it was, her face was covered in the soft brown feathers of the Owl, who had perched on her shoulder.

The touch of the Owl seemed to have driven away her grief, and she felt quite light and joyful in the beautiful sunshine. For it seemed as if the Owl had become a companion to her that would take the place of her father; so she leaned her head against the Owl, and her golden hair mixed with the dusky brown feathers, till each streak of golden hair shone again in the bright sunlight. And the Owl too seemed very happy. So for a time the Princess stood looking over the deep-blue sea.

Suddenly, however, a footstep sounded in the courtyard below, and the Princess drew back from the window, for a thought suddenly came into her head :

'Oh dear,' she said, 'I have been crying such a lot that my eyes must be quite red, and my hair is all ruffled. This will never do.' And as she looked in the glass she said, 'Ah, just as I thought. Come, my cherished Owl, sit there on the crown on the top of the looking-glass frame and wait while I wash my hands and face and make myself tidy.'

The Owl did as he was told, and the Princess began to wash in cold water— a thing she had never done before— but she did not like to call to her ladies-in-waiting, lest they should see how red her eyes were. So she had to put up with the cold water, and very pleasant she found it, for it cleared the tear-mist out of her eyes and made her feel quite happy and cheerful again: 'And I have heard,' she thought to herself, 'that washing in

cold water is matchless for the com-
plexion.'

When she had finished washing she
went and combed her hair before the
glass. For she was a very artistic
Princess, and liked looking at beautiful
things, and so she liked sometimes to
look at herself in the glass. Not that
she was in the least conceited.

So she combed her hair with a gold
comb, and when she had finished
combing it, she put on her gold circlet
as a sign of her rank, and then she
said to the Owl, who had been sitting
patiently on the looking-glass blinking
at her as if he quite enjoyed himself:

'Now, cherished Owl, you may sit
on my shoulder again.'

When the Owl was again in his
place he blinked in the glass at his
own reflection as if the light were too
strong for him, and he shut his eyes
and drew in his neck and lifted up one
foot into his feathers, as if he felt quite
happy and comfortable, and the Prin-

cess smiled at his happy look, for she seemed quite to have forgotten her sorrow in the company of the Owl.

So she, with the Owl on her shoulder, went to the window.   Here in the courtyard already a large crowd had collected to catch a glimpse of the Princess if possible, so that it fell about that when they saw her they raised a mighty shout of joy and pity :

'The King is dead,' they cried. 'Long live the Queen !'   And throughout the city far and wide echoed and re-echoed the cry :

'Long live the Queen'; and it seemed as if the waves of the sea murmured the sound.

The Princess, however, held out her little hand to still the tumult, and as if by magic the cries stopped.

'Good people all,' she said in clear ringing tones, 'I thank you for your good wishes, and I will try always to be worthy of them as my father was. For to-day, however, rejoice not;

remember that the great King Intafernes, the founder of the kingdom to
which we all belong, has but just left
the earth—sorrow for him but a short
time; joy will come soon enough for
all.'

So the crowd, silent and pensive for
a time, dispersed in groups. More
than one of them asked what had been
perched on the Princess's shoulder,
and those who had been near enough,
said that it was an owl—though what
it meant they knew not.

'To me it seemed as if the head of
the old King were looking over his
daughter's shoulder,' said one of the
listeners who stood on the outskirts of
the crowd.

But she was only a little hunchback,
and the rich citizens laughed at her,
saying : 'Tush, child—thy fancy is not
sound ! Or else before looking at the
Princess thou didst look at the fierce
sun, and the sun-spots in thy eyes
caused thee to see it thus. It was

but an owl.' But the little hunchback
held to her own opinion.

But while the Princess stood watching them depart, a tapping came at
the door, and the Princess cried 'Come
in.' A page entered and said that the
Chancellor, Merrymineral, was below
and requested audience of the Princess.

'Let him be shown into the audience
chamber to await me there.'

The page bowed and departed on
his errand, and the Princess went to
another door in the room and down
the staircase that led from it to the
audience chamber, and the Owl remained seated on her shoulder until
they reached the room. When they
got there the Chancellor had not yet
entered, for the staircase from the
Princess's bedroom to the audience
chamber was much shorter than
that from the entrance hall, and then
you see the Princess was much more
nimble than Merrymineral, who was an
old man, and she ran quickly down-

stairs whilst he walked slowly up. However at last he entered. As he came in the Princess said :

'Good morning, dear Merrymineral. How is it you are so late? I shall have to fine you if you keep me waiting like this again. And now what do you want with me?'

The good Chancellor received her laughing reproach with his head bowed down. He heaved a deep sigh, and drew his pocket-handkerchief from his pocket and applied it to his eyes. As he drew it away the tears could be seen flowing fast down his withered cheeks.

'I came,' he moaned, 'to console you for your great loss. I too,' he continued in a voice choked with sobs, 'I too am an orphan.'

It seemed funny to the Princess to see him weeping thus, and she could hardly help laughing at him, but her grief soon came back.

'Poor Merrymineral,' she sighed,

'to you also it must be a sad blow, for you were always faithful and attached. But it was fated to happen thus, and you must really try and be comforted, for crying will not mend matters.'

The Chancellor began again :

'The beloved King your father'; but his sobs choked him, and he hid his face.

'The beloved King your father,' echoed a loud voice, exactly mimicking the tones of the Chancellor, but where the voice came from no one could tell. The Chancellor started.

'Did you say that?' said the Princess.

'Not the second time,' answered Merrymineral.

'Who could it be?' said the Princess; 'for there is no one in the room except the cherished Owl; and you can't speak, can you, Owl dear?'

The Owl shook his head dismally. But the change that came over Merry-

mineral was most astonishing as his
eye suddenly lit upon the Owl—for
since his entrance he had not raised
his eyes from the floor. He jumped ,
backwards over three rows of seats, for
you see the seats in the audience
chamber were arranged in rows, and he
alighted in a sitting posture on the
other side. As he sat on the floor he
looked up at the Owl in a terrified
manner, then threw up his arms and
fainted. The poor Princess did not
know what to do, so she rang a bell
that stood on the table in front of the
throne. Several pages at once came in.

'Just bring that man to,' said the
Princess.

The pages bowed low, and went and
shook the Chancellor violently. He
showed no signs of recovering, so one
of the pages turned to the Princess
and said :

'May it please your Majesty, but the
Chancellor refuses to come to, and we
can't bring him.'

'So he refuses to obey my orders,' said the Princess. 'He must be punished for this. However, now go and get a bucketful of water and pour it on him. Perhaps that will bring him to.'

Now when she said he was to be punished, she was only joking, but she said it very gravely, so that many people might have thought it was quite in earnest. Meanwhile the pages departed to fetch the water. They soon came back and brought a large pailful.

'You had better not throw it all over him,' said the Princess; 'just let it trickle over his face gently.'

So one of the pages began to do as he was told, but somehow—either he had a sudden push, or, as he said afterwards, the Owl looked at him, and startled him—he let the pail go, and all the water and the pail too fell over the unlucky Chancellor. This really did bring him very much to—much too much to, in fact—for he sprang up in such a rage that the Princess really wished herself out of the room.

'You jackanapes,' he screamed at the unfortunate page; 'you ape, you boar, you cow, you clumsy monkey, I'll be revenged on you.'

But the Princess, who had gained courage while he was screaming, said:

'You will not be revenged on him.'

'But I shall,' he said.

'Indeed you will not,' said the Princess, 'for he did it by my orders.'

'Oh! he did it by your orders,' said the Chancellor; 'then I'll be revenged on you too,' and he began to move uncomfortably near to the Princess. But the three pages threw themselves on him and tried to drag him back, but he turned suddenly on them.

'What,' he said scornfully, 'you try to stop me—ye frogs! Ah! a good idea—by virtue of my magic power I command you to turn into water-rats;

then perhaps the Owl there will eat you up.'

No sooner said than done, and the three pages instantly became water-rats, squattering in the water that was still in a pool on the floor.

Somehow the Princess did not seem to be at all frightened at this; she was only very angry.

'I thought I told you not to hurt those pages.'

'Who cares what you say?'

'Dear me,' thought the Princess, 'he is getting excessively insolent—I shall have to be severe with him in a moment.' So she said:

'Turn those pages back again.'

'I shall not.'

'Then leave the room.'

'I shall not.'

The Princess did not know what to do; he was really very rude, and he was walking towards her evidently intending to attack her. When he was within ten feet of her he stopped,

and though he tried to get nearer he
could not.

'Ha! ha!' he cried; 'you think to
keep me off by magic, but it is not so
easy, I can tell you. By virtue of my
magic power I command you to turn
into a mouse.'

But the Princess, leaning her head
against the soft feathers of the Owl,
only smiled, and did not turn into a
mouse at all.

The Chancellor seemed perplexed.

'Is that not enough for you?' he
said; 'I thought I told you to turn
into a mouse.'

But the Princess smiled calmly and
said:

'Do you suppose I am going to
do anything of the sort—you have
forgotten your manners to speak to
your Queen thus. I believe there is
a fine of five shillings for any one who
speaks to the King or Queen without
saying "Your Majesty." You had better
pay it, Sir Chancellor, and turn those

pages back again, or I shall have you turned out of the kingdom.'

But the Chancellor laughed. 'You can't send me out if you wanted to. Meanwhile I shall not turn those rats back, for if I am not much mistaken your Owl there will carry them off.'

It really seemed as if the Owl were going to obey him, for greatly to the Princess's surprise it sprang off her shoulder and seized the three rats, one in each claw, and one in its beak— but it returned at once to her and laid them squeaking on the table in front of her—but no sooner did they touch the table than they turned into men again just as quickly as they had become rats. When Merrymineral saw this he became perfectly frantic, and tried in vain to get at the Princess —he even went back a little and tried to run at her—but it was no use, for no sooner did he reach a certain spot than he was suddenly stopped, just as if he had run against a wall. At last he became so frantic that the Princess could stand it no longer. So she said :

'Will you be quiet, you naughty old man?—leave the room or I will send for the police.'

But Merrymineral answered :

'Oh, send for the police and the soldiers and sailors and candlestick-makers.'

So the Princess rang the bell that stood on the table: a page at once appeared at the door.

'Send for a policeman and ask him to step this way.'

The page looked astonished, but he saluted and left the room. Almost immediately a policeman came in—for you see there was one always on the palace steps. He entered the room with a low bow.

'Take the Chancellor out of the room,' said the Princess, 'and put him in prison for three days.'

But the policeman shook his head.

D

'Excuse me, mum—I mean your most gracious Majesty — but it is against the law to imprison a member of Parliament, much less a chancellor.'

The Chancellor laughed sarcastically.

'Oh, is it?' said the Princess; 'never mind, take him into custody; I depose him—he is no longer Chancellor.'

Merrymineral looked astonished, but the policeman cleared his throat and said:

'Come, I say, young fellow; will you go quietly, or shall I make you?'

'Oh, make me, by all means,' answered Merrymineral.

So the policeman advanced and held out his hand to take him by the collar, but had no sooner touched Merrymineral than he fell to the ground as if he had been thunderstruck.

The Chancellor smiled. 'I told you so,' he said.

The Princess was now thoroughly

nonplussed. However, she rang the bell again. Again the page appeared.

'Summon the Lords of the Council; let them come here at once.'

Almost immediately afterwards the lords appeared. As they came in each one bowed profoundly to the Princess. But in spite of their grave appearance they could not help looking astonished at the policeman, who was lying on the floor, and at the three pages who were still sitting on the table—for as they had not yet been told to go they could not depart.

But each one took his seat without questioning. Last of all came the Court doctor, who looked in an alarmed manner at the Owl—nevertheless he took his seat.

When all was quiet the Princess began to speak.

'My lords,' she said, 'I have been obliged to assemble you on the first day of my reign; but the matter is a very grave one. I have found it necessary to dismiss the Chancellor, for these reasons : first, he attacked these three pages who were executing my bidding ; next, he attacked me ; and lastly, he attacked the law, in the person of the policeman there, whom he knocked down. Now I ask your advice as to how I am to get rid of him, for he refuses to leave the room at my command.'

So spoke the Princess, but before any one could answer Merrymineral spoke :

' My lords,' he said, ' are we, we, the lords of the kingdom, to be governed by this schoolgirl, who is not even a magician as we are ? What good has she ever done us ? What power is to keep us from deposing her and electing as a ruler one of ourselves ? '—— but before he could finish a perfect uproar of shouts of rage interrupted him.

The Princess put her fingers in her ears to keep out the sound, and when the lords saw that the noise was annoying her they stopped at once.

When they were quiet the Princess spoke again :

'What he has just said is right,' she said; 'I have no right to reign over you, for I am but a girl. Do ye therefore elect a ruler.'

For a moment all was silence in the Council, but all eyes were turned on a lord who stood next to Merrymineral in rank. He was a portly man, and a great magician too, though his power was not quite so great as Merrymineral's. When therefore he saw that all eyes were turned on him, Lord Licec, for so he was called, rose.

'Your most gracious Majesty,' he began, 'although you had no need to command us to elect a ruler, we are of course bound to obey your commands, whatever they are. I therefore speak, giving my vote, and I believe the vote of all the rest of the assembly, that you shall be our ruler according to the oath which we sware to your father.'

And then turning to the rest of the assembly he said :

'Am I not right, my lords?' and with one voice they answered :

'We will die for our Queen Ismara.'

Only one voice objected, but as that was Merrymineral, no one noticed him.

So the Princess rose and thanked them for their confidence in her, though, to tell the truth, she had known all along what they would say. That done she said :

'And now what are we to do about turning this man out? for he refuses to go of his own accord.'

No one could suggest anything better than to send for the Lifeguards and let them carry him off. But before this was done they decided to try to persuade him to go. But it was of no use, for he stood on the spot where he had stopped, with his arms folded and his hat on, looking down at the ground in a brown study, and he took no notice of anything they could do, even though they rang the bell close to his ear. Now he did no particular harm as he stood there, but you see no one could tell whom he might attack next. So they determined to send for the Lifeguards as a last resource.

So they were sent for, and in a short time they came, although they left their horses outside in the courtyard. Fifty of them were then marched into the hall and they were ordered to move the man out. So they divided into two parties of twenty-five each, and they put a rope round him, and each body of twenty-five took an end of the rope and pulled, but it was no good, for he took no more notice of the pulling than if he had been Samson or any other strong man. So the fifty gave up the attempt in despair; the only thing to do seemed to be to cut him to pieces. So they drew their swords and hacked at him,

but it was no use : the swords bent or .
broke just as if they had been bul-
rushes or paper, and still Merrymineral
took no notice in particular. So they
gave up the attempt in despair when
they had broken up all their swords.
However, they did not give in, for they
called in the best horseman in the
regiment and told him to charge on
horseback with his lance in rest. So
the soldier rode in on his horse ; this
was not so difficult as it may seem, for
the council chamber was on a level
with the ground, and a lane was opened
in between the chairs to where Merry·
mineral still stood with his arms folded.

At the word of command the soldier
rode at full speed towards Merrymineral, aiming his lance at the centre
of his face—that is his nose. His
aim was true, and the lance hit fair,
but it might just as well have been
made of macaroni, for it crumbled
just as a stick of that delightful eatable
would do if you ran it against a wall.

The horse, however, swerved just in time, although it pushed against him in going by; but even this made no difference to Merrymineral. As a last resource they suggested putting a lighted match under his nose. Whether this would have succeeded or not I can't say. But just at this moment Merrymineral seemed to wake up again.

'Ah,' he said, 'I see you have not yet managed to get me out of the room. However, as your soldiers have been practising on me for some time past, I think it only right that I should try my hand on them a little. I used to be thought rather strong in the arms at one time, and I have cut down a good many trees in my time. Just see how you like that,' he said to the man on the horse as he swung his umbrella round his head and brought it down with a tremendous thwack on the horse's side. In fact he hit so hard that the horse and man were knocked right through the window into the courtyard below. With three more blows he knocked twenty more of the men through the same window, and the rest made their escape as fast as they could by the door.

'I see I have not quite forgotten how to clear a room yet,' he said, as he once more folded his arms in the same attitude and relapsed into silence.

'What *am* I to do?' said the poor Princess, wringing her hands and almost crying with vexation.

A voice came from the far end of the room, and every one turned to see who it might be. And all saw it was the Court physician who spoke. 'If I might be allowed to make a suggestion,' he said, 'I would say that the best thing your Majesty could do would be to request that gentleman who is sitting on your shoulder to turn him out. From my own experience I should say he was very competent to

perform such a task. And if I might
be allowed to add yet another suggestion it would be, "to be well shaken
before taken," as they say in prescrip-
tions.'

As he said this an extraordinary
change came over Merrymineral. He
pressed his hat on his head, put his
umbrella under his arm, and began to
put on his gloves in such a hurry that
he mistook the left for the right hand.
As he did so he said :

'Do you know, I can't stop any
longer ; so sorry, but I have an engage-
ment and I am rather in a hurry.
Good-day.' And he began to walk
quickly towards the door. But the
Princess had already whispered to
the Owl, 'Catch him, dear Owl.'

And however fast he went the Owl
caught him up, and taking him by the
middle of his coat-tails—and I am
bound to say some of his skin too—he
shook him violently, and flew round
and round the room banging him

violently against any high piece of furniture that was convenient.

'O-o-o-h,' shrieked the wretched man, 'I say, do you know you're tearing my best coat, and your beak is awfully sharp? O-o-ouch,' and he filled the room with his shrieks. After they had continued like that for some minutes the Princess said :

'I think he has been punished enough now, cherished Owl, so let him down.'

The Owl did as he was told, not, however, without giving him a sly tweak with his bill that must have hurt him a good deal.

'I'll be revenged on you,' roared Merrymineral; 'you've spoilt my Sunday coat, and I shan't be able to afford another for I don't know how long. I'll be revenged on you.' And he took out a red pocket-handkerchief and began to suage the blood that was coming from the bite, all the while abusing the Owl and the Princess and threatening to be revenged.

'You had better be quiet and go,' she said.

'I shall not.'

'Oh, very well,' she answered, 'perhaps you would like to try the Owl again.'

At the same time the Owl gave him such a look from its gleaming eyes that he turned first red and then white with fright. He made a dash for the window, and he was in such a hurry that he left his umbrella and one of his gloves behind him.

He jumped right through the window high into the air, and as soon as he got outside, strange to say, he began to burn furiously, and he went gradually up into the sky like a fire-balloon—just as when a piece of tissue paper is put on the fire, if you are not careful, it will fly blazing up the chimney.

They watched him out of sight, and then the Princess said with a little sigh of relief:

'That's an end of him at last.'

But the Owl shook his head—he knew better.

When he was thus at last got rid off the Princess said to the physician:

'How can we ever thank thee enough, good doctor, for thy timely suggestion!'

'Oh, your Majesty,' said the blushing doctor, 'experience does it; and I had plenty of that this morning. Do you know, I think I shall never be free again from pain—although I have bathed in opodeldoc and arnica, and I am clothed from head to foot in Court plaster.'

The Princess smiled and said:

'I am afraid the Owl is a little over-vigorous in such matters; however, I will give orders to the Court apothecary to supply you with remedies at my expense until you shall be cured.' She then said to the three pages who still sat on the table:

'I must ask you to depart now as Parliament cannot carry on business with strangers in the house. However, ye are, I believe, pages; I will turn over a new leaf and will advance you each a step in rank. Now, however, go.'

Thanking her profusely they went. When they had gone the Princess turned to the Councillors and said:

'As there seems no further need to keep you, I will detain you no longer.'

Having her permission the Councillors left the hall. Last of all was Lord Licec, and he remained as if hesitating whether to go, or to stay and speak to the Princess. She, noticing his hesitation, said:

'Ah, Lord Licec, hast thou something to ask me?'

The old lord made answer:

'I would ask your Majesty's permission to enter the room of the late King, your Majesty's father, for, as you are aware, it is against the law to enter the royal presence without the royal permission.'

'You have my permission of course; but ought not some preparations to be made for the funeral?'

Lord Licec answered:

'They are already made. For as the late King had announced his intention of dying yesterday at half-past six P.M., there was ample time.'

'Let us then go together to the room, my lord,' said the Princess.

So they went together, the Princess leaning on Licec's arm, and the Owl sitting on her shoulder.

The guards of the room saluted as they passed in, but what was their astonishment on entering to find that the King had disappeared. When they asked the guards who had come into the room during the day, they replied that no one had been near the room during their watch, and the guards of the watch before said exactly the same thing. All over the palace inquiries were made, but to no purpose, and the rumour gradually spread to the town,

and throngs of anxious citizens flocked about the palace gates to ask, but neither they nor any one else ever heard what had become of him, and it is my opinion that the King himself is the only person who knew anything about it. It came out in the course of inquiries that when the attendants had rushed in on hearing the Princess's call for assistance the night before, they had not seen the King on the bed, but in his place had sat an enormous owl, and this owl had insisted on accompanying the Princess wherever she went.

This was the first time that the Princess had heard of how the Owl had come to her, but still she had known all along that the Owl was the one her father had made her promise to cherish. But there were ill-natured people who said that it was not so very unlikely that the Owl had eaten the King up, but the Princess only laughed and said :

E

'How could the Owl eat a king up when the poor thing has so little appetite that it only eats very small pieces of meat off my golden fork at dinner?'

And so the Owl remained with the Princess: during the day it always sat on her shoulder, or took short flights round her head, and at night it slept on the foot of her bed.

So six weeks glided peacefully away, and everything prospered; but one day a terrified messenger rode into the city at full speed, and the message that he brought was this.

Merrymineral, who, as the Owl had said, was by no means done with, had been inciting the people of far-off lands such as Mesopotamia and Padan-Aram and Ireland to rebel, and he was now marching against the Princess at the head of an immense army, laying waste the country for miles around. At the rate he was coming, however, it would take him a fortnight

to get near the country round. So
you see there was no immediate
danger; still an enemy's army could
not be allowed to remain in the
country unopposed. So the Princess
gave Lord Licec the order to assemble
the army, and, as you may imagine,
it was an immense one when it did
assemble. I can't say how large it
was, but if you could have stood on a
hill in the centre of the town you
would have seen nothing for miles
around but shining silk banners and
glistening helmets and lances. Never
before had the world held such an
army, and it never will again. Yet this
army even was hardly as large as that
of the enemy. The command of the
army was given to Lord Licec, for he
was well known to be the most prudent
man in the kingdom.

Three days passed till the last of
the army had started, and all the while
the Princess stood at the window and
watched them march along the wind-

ing street below, and the knights and
men-at-arms were inspired with fresh
courage at the sight of such a princess
as they had to defend, and they
cheered so loud and long that it
seemed like the continual roar of the
sea beating on a rocky shore, sometimes rising, sometimes falling, but
always sounding.

The Princess indeed felt quite
lonely when they had all gone, even
though their shouts did make her
head ache. However, she consoled
herself by riding all day towards the
army, and returning at night to the
lonely town. So she occupied three
days; and the Owl always flew over
her head, protecting her from the sun
when it was too hot, or else sitting on
her shoulder, or on the horse's head,
although the horse did not like it at all.

For three days no news came, but
on the fourth as the Princess was
riding out with her ladies-in-waiting
she saw at a great distance in front of

her along the straight white road a cloud of dust that was coming swiftly towards her. As it came nearer she could see the glint of armour, and soon she could plainly see the form of an armed knight galloping at full speed towards them. He came so fast that they had to rein their horses to one side that they might not be run down. At first he did not seem to know who the Princess was, or perhaps he was going so furiously that he could not see; at any rate he had almost got past them before he recognised her. As soon as he did, however, he drew up, but so sudden was the action that the horse first sank back on his haunches, and then bounded so high into the air that the marks that his hoofs made when he alighted on the ground again, were a foot deep in the hard road. As soon as the plunging of the horse stopped and the Princess could make herself heard she said :

'What news, Sir Knight, from the front, that thou ridest in such haste?

'But bad news, I fear,' answered the knight.

'What say you?' said the Princess; 'bad news, and with such an army as ye had? has some fresh rebellion broken out among the men?'

'No rebellion, but plain fighting has beaten us—but what can we do against such foes? This Merrymineral, alone, rides on a green dragon, and with one stroke of his sword he kills a hundred men. Myself I charged him with my lance, but as it struck his shield it broke in pieces as if it had been made of glass; and it was fortunate for me that my horse carried me past him before he could strike me, for I saw him myself cut the Knight of Pendred in half, as you would cut a radish. And if we slay a thousand men during the day he restores them in the night. So we have gradually been driven back, till after three days'

fighting the army remains at Arecarp.
Thence I started at eight this morn-
ing to hurry the reinforcements from
Britain and Gaul.'

'Alas! they are still at three days'
march from here, though they are
marching night and day. But thou
saidst the army was at Arecarp, and
that thou didst start to-day at eight in
the morning. That is impossible.
Arecarp is twenty-four hours' journey
for a fast horse, and it is now but
twelve o'clock. Not even the horse
that I ride could go faster than that,
though he is said to be the fastest horse
in the world, except Selim, the horse of
the Prince of India. However, no
time is to be lost. Sir Knight, will you
escort these ladies back to the town,
and rest for a while?'

'But what will you do, your
Majesty?

'I must ride forward to Arecarp.'

'To Arecarp! Your Majesty, what

will you do there? The battlefield is no place for a girl.'

'Nevertheless I must go, for my place is with the army.'

'But if you are killed what will happen to your people without their Queen?'

'What do they do now without their Queen? Besides once before the cherished Owl has defeated this man and he may do it again. If he does not, no power on earth could save me from death, for the army is being gradually defeated.'

'But your Majesty could send the Owl in a cage against the enemy.'

'I promised my father never to go out of its sight—no, I must go.'

'I beseech you then, your Majesty, to allow me to accompany you, for the road to the camp is full of danger.'

'But your horse is tired, and even if he were not he could never keep up with me.'

'But if you will excuse the con-
tradiction, I think I shall.'

'Well then, have your own way, but
mark me, if you lag behind I shall not
stop. However, we are losing time.
Let us go.'

And they set off—the Princess
ignoring the entreaties of the ladies
that she should not go.

The Princess immediately started at
the full speed of her horse, expecting
that the knight would soon fall behind ;
but no, he galloped at her side as if
the speed were not more than usual,
and his great black charger seemed to
enjoy the exercise as though he had not
already galloped over a hundred miles
that morning.

The Princess could not understand
how it was, but she thought he would
soon get tired and fall behind, but
an hour passed and he showed no
signs of being fatigued. So she
leant over her horse and whispered
softly in his ear. Instantly the horse

bounded forward more swiftly than
ever—so fast, indeed, that she could
hardly keep her eyes open against the
wind, and her golden crown was
suddenly whisked away, and her
beautiful golden hair streamed far out
behind. Still the knight kept up, and
seemed not the least distressed at the
speed. The Owl meanwhile was fly-
ing far overhead, but she was not at all
surprised at his keeping up, for nothing seemed impossible to him. After
they had been riding thus for nearly
two hours they came to a place where
the path was crossed by a river, and
here the Princess thought it advisable
to stop and rest a moment and to let
the horses drink. So she called to
the knight to stop, as she was going
to get off for a moment, and he at
once sprang off his horse, and coming
to her saddle-bow held her stirrup for
her to dismount. When she was off
she leaned against a tree looking at
the horses as they drank eagerly from

the river, and then came out to browse
for a moment on the bank.   Then she
went to where the knight's horse stood,
and patted him on the neck, for you see
he was not a very fierce-looking animal,
and she was not at all afraid of him.

'He's a wonderfully swift horse, Sir
Knight,' she said suddenly, 'and I
believe there is no other horse in the
world as swift—not even Selim—the
horse I spoke about—that belongs to
the Prince of India.'

The knight nodded.

'He is a good horse, but he is no
better than Selim, your Majesty, for I
know Selim very well.'

All this while he had kept his vizor
down, and the Princess had been too
polite to ask him to raise it, even
though it was rather rude of him to
keep it down.   So she could not tell
who he was.   She knew all the knights
of her own kingdom by sight, as well as
most of her allies, for you must know
that a great many foreign princes had

sent her troops to assist her against the rebel. She looked at the device on his shield; it was a crowned tiger, but that did not help her, for she did not know whose crest it was. So at last when she could bear her curiosity no longer, she determined to ask him. So she said:

'Sir Knight, should you think me very rude if I were to ask you whether you are under a vow of hiding your face?'

'I am bound by no such vow; but why do you ask, your Majesty?'

'Because ever since I have seen you you have kept your vizor down, and I thought perhaps it was on account of some such vow.'

'Oh, I beg your pardon a thousand times, your Majesty,' said the knight. 'But I did not remember that I had let it down, for you see I look through its bars without noticing the difference. But I hope your Majesty will pardon the absent-mindedness,' and he raised the vizor, at the same time bowing low to her. But it was now the Princess's turn to be confused, for she saw before her Sir Alured the Emperor of India, a prince nearly as powerful as herself. She blushed with shame and then said:

'Oh, Sir Knight, I mean your Royal Highness, it is I who should crave your pardon, for all the while I have addressed you as "Sir Knight," instead of as "your Majesty." But I am very · sorry.'

But Sir Alured said :

'Nay, your Majesty, you have the right to call me what you will, for I am always your humble vassal.'

'My ally, you should say, your Majesty.'

'I am always your servant, not your ally, your Majesty.'

'Then I fear you will soon be the vassal of a queen without a kingdom ; and if this Merrymineral prevail over me, I fear he will punish you for having aided me.'

But the Prince said :

'All is not yet lost, your Majesty, and whatever happens your Majesty will always have a protector while I am alive.'

The Princess smiled.

'Ah! you mean the cherished Owl. You will always protect me, won't you, Owl?' she said, looking up at the Owl who was seated again on her shoulder. And the Owl nodded his head.

She looked at her watch just then. 'Why,' she said, 'we have been here just ten minutes, and it is time to start again, if you are rested sufficiently.'

So he helped her to mount, and they crossed the river. It was not very deep, but still she got the skirts of her dress quite wet, for the water was high enough for that.

However, the gallop in the hot sun on the other side soon dried them.

In an hour and a half they were on the top of a hill from which they could see the town of Arecarp in the valley beneath.

The sun was shining brightly on the tents of the army as it lay round the town, and at some distance the camp of the enemy appeared. But still all looked peaceful.

The Prince gazed carefully at the armies. After a moment he said:

'There has been no fighting since I left the city this morning, nor has the position altered at all. I fancy Merrymineral has sent ambassadors to demand surrender from Lord Licec.'

The Princess smiled.

'He will never surrender,' she said.

'Nor will any of us, your Majesty,' added the Prince. 'However, let us descend the hill.'

Down the hill the road lay through a deep gorge, so deep that the sun did not penetrate it, and it lay in delicious shade. The sides of the valley were lined with the silver-barked birch, below which grew nodding foxgloves, and as they went slowly down the steep path, ever and anon a rabbit would scuttle out of the grassy track to a safe distance in front of them, where it sat on its haunches with its little ears pricked up, smelling at them anxiously as they came near again, and then it would scutter along into the thick rank grass to its home.

So they went slowly down the path until they came once more to the level ground, and they were again able to gallop on.

Soon they reached the town, and clattered through the cobbled streets to the market-place, where Lord Licec had his head-quarters. But the market-place was crowded with soldiers and knights who were bargaining for food, so that it was by no means easy to get through the crowd. However, as soon as they got near the place, the soldiers recognised the Princess and began to cheer, and immediately an avenue was formed up to the door of the council-house, and the Princess rode smiling through the throng, followed by the Prince.

The news of her arrival ran through the whole camp, and immediately such a shout went up from the men that the enemy thought they were preparing for battle, and they made ready to resist the attack. At the door of the council-hall Lord Licec was waiting with the rest of the captains of renown, and they followed the Princess upstairs to the council-chamber.

As soon as they were seated the Princess asked for the latest news. She was told all that had happened, and when she had heard it she dismissed the Lords of the Council, all except Lord Licec and the Prince of India, who were to stay and dine with her, and she gave orders that the dinner should be brought as soon as possible, for to tell the truth she felt rather hungry, as she had had nothing to eat since breakfast-time.

Now when the Princess had finished

F

giving her orders about the dinner, Licec could not refrain from asking her why she had come.

'Was it not rather foolish,' he said, 'to hazard your life for nothing? for of a truth you are——'

But the Princess put her finger on his mouth.

'I will not be bullied by you, my lord, even though you are old enough to be my father. I know what you were going to say—that the battlefield is no place for girls. Now I won't be called a girl, for I'm nineteen, you know. His Majesty the Emperor of India there insulted me by calling me a girl, and I have not forgiven him yet. Besides you'll spoil my appetite for dinner if you lecture me. It always does; so do be quiet now, at any rate till after dinner.'

So Licec had to be quiet, and they talked about something else till dinner-time.

Just as they had finished, a frightful

shouting outside made them drop their dessert knives and run to the window, but as the window did not face on to the street they could not tell what was the matter. So the Princess rang the bell, and when the servant appeared she asked him what was the cause of the shouting.

'May it please your Majesty, ambassadors have arrived from the enemy and would speak to you.'

'Show them this way and send at the same time for the Lords of the Council.'

So the servant went, and in a short time a heavy stumping was heard on the stairs. Suddenly the door burst open and the ambassadors entered. They were a rather remarkable pair of ambassadors, although they could hardly be said to pair well. For the one was an enormous giant with a long beard, dressed in leaves mostly, and so tall that he could not stand upright in the room; in his hand he carried an enormous pole, from the end of which a spiked. ball dangled. The other, however, was very nearly his opposite in everything. For he was very small, a dwarf in fact, and he was dressed in very tight yellow armour, and from the top of his helmet a crest of red roses hung down to his saddle— for you must know he had insisted on not getting off his horse, or rather pony, for that too was very small—in fact it just fitted the dwarf.

As soon as the Princess had re-covered from her astonishment, she rose from her seat and said :

' Are you the ambassadors from the rebel Merrymineral ?'

The dwarf replied :

' I don't know anything about the rebel part of the business, but we are the ambassadors from Merrymineral, whom we are bound to serve for a certain time. But who are you, I should like to know, and what right have you to speak to me in this insulting manner? D'you think I'm here to be insulted by you? If you think so, I'll tell you point-blank I'm not—so there.' And in the rage he had worked himself into he began to spur his steed till it jumped off the floor so high that it knocked his head against the ceiling.

The Princess was not used to being treated like that. However she was not at all angry at it—she only laughed at his misfortune, which made him all the more outrageous.

'How dare you laugh at me?' he screamed; 'who are you, you minx, you minx, you lynx—you——'

But the Princess did not listen to him. She turned to the giant, who at any rate was quiet, and said:

'Will you not take a chair until the Lords of the Council arrive?'

The giant looked at her in stupid astonishment.

'What shall I do with the chair when I've taken it?' he mumbled.

'I mean you to sit down on it, of course,' said the Princess.

The giant growled out in reply :   .

'Well, I never sat on a chair before, but to please you I will.'

So he sat down, but as he was not used to sitting on chairs he sat down on its back; but it was only a small cane-bottomed chair, and as he was very big, and the chair was very small, the result is easily foreseen, for the chair collapsed under him as if he had sat on a top-hat, and he reclined comfortably on the floor, where he remained for the rest of the time.

'I think I'll stop where I am,' he said, when they offered him a wooden stool to sit on, 'for you see I'm not used to chairs.' So they let him stop where he was.

One by one the Lords of the Council began to arrive ; they looked curiously at the ambassadors but said nothing. When they were all arrived the Princess said to the dwarf :

'Now if you will state your message we will listen.'

So the dwarf snarled in a bad-tempered voice :

'I shan't tell you—you aren't the commander-in-chief of the army, are you ?'

'No, but I am the Queen of the Western World.'

'Oh ! you're the Queen of the Western World, are you ? Well, you won't be Queen of the Western World long, if you don't mind your P's and Q's. The king Merrymineral sent me to say that if you don't marry him and make him king, he'll kill the lot of you and make himself king in spite of you—so there ; and I'm to wait for an answer.'

After consulting the Council for a moment the Princess said :

'Of course I shan't marry him—how could he be so ridiculous as to think so ?'

The dwarf laughed.

'That's your answer, is it?' he said. 'I thought so. I say, Gog, have you written it down?'

But Gog had gone to sleep. So the dwarf pricked him with the end of his lance.

'I say, Gog,' he said, 'she's given her answer and you haven't written it down, and I've forgotten it already. Just say it over again, Queen, will you? and not too fast, or Gog here will never get it down.'

The giant now drew from his pocket a very soiled and crumpled half-sheet of a copy-book and began to write from the Princess's dictation.

'Of course I should not do anything so——' Here he stopped.

'How do you spell "ridiculous"?' he said.

'With two "k's," of course,' said the dwarf; 'even I know that, though I can't write.'

When he had finished he handed it to the Princess:

' Just sign your name, will you ? '

The Princess signed her name, but she could not help seeing that the writing was very bad and the spelling was awful.

'Why didn't they send some one who could write better? Why! that " r " is more like a " k " than an " r ".'

But the giant shook his head mournfully.

' They hadn't got any one else in the army who could write except Merrymineral, and he was afraid to come.'

' But weren't you afraid to come?' she said.

The giant shook his mace round so violently that it grazed the helmet of the dwarf, and cut his crest of roses off.

'Whom am I to be afraid of?' he growled. 'I could kill your whole army single-handed'; and he laughed loud and long.

But just at this moment the Owl, that had been sitting on the floor behind the Princess's chair, flew up on to her shoulder, and no sooner did the giant see the Owl than he jumped up from the floor, where you remember he was sitting, and he was in such a hurry that he knocked a hole in the plaster of the ceiling with his head.

'Come, I say, you know,' he said, 'I can fight anything in reason—but I'm not going to tackle that, you know; besides, we're ambassadors, and you can't hurt us. I'm going'; and he rushed out of the room as fast as he could, and the dwarf followed him as fast as he could make his horse gallop, and they never stopped till they reached the camp of Merrymineral. For they were very frightened, you see.

After they had gone the Princess again dismissed the Councillors, and when they had gone, she said to Lord Licec and the Prince, who by the bye still remained :

'Now let us finish our dessert'—for

the ambassadors had come in right in the middle of it.

After a moment the Princess said :

'How absurd of him to think I would marry him — why, he's old enough to be my great-grandfather.'

But suddenly she became grave :

'But perhaps I ought to have thought before I gave the answer. Would it not have been better for my people if I had consented ? for then he would kill no more of them.'

But the Prince became quite angry at such an idea. 'It's absurd,' he said. 'Why, as soon as he had married you and become king he would murder you and then kill just as many of your people as he will now'; besides, who knows that we may not still conquer him ?'

The Princess turned to Lord Licec :

'What do you say, my lord?' she said.

'I think just as the Prince of India —for even if he did not murder you he would oppress the people without mercy, and besides, your people would never allow you to marry him, so that is out of the question.'

The Princess gave a sigh of relief.

'Since you say so, Lord Licec, it must be right; besides, I don't think I could ever marry him—he is such a very unpleasant sort of man.'

And the Prince answered:

'You are quite right there'; and he seemed quite happy again.

Soon after it became evening, and Lord Licec had to go out to look after his army, and the Prince too went to see that his men were all prepared for any night attack—for his men were right in the very front of all, and so they were quite close to the enemy, who might at any time begin an attack.

So the Princess was left all alone with the Owl, but she did not feel lonely with him, for he was very sociable, and would do anything that he was told to do. So they played hide-and-seek till it was too dark to see any more, and then she went to bed and slept soundly till the rays of the sun falling on her face the next morning woke her up. She was soon dressed, and when she had finished she went into the next room, where she found Lord Licec already awaiting her.

'What does your Majesty intend to do this morning? for I shall not be with you, as I am going to order the army to advance to the attack, and so your Majesty had better stay within the town for the rest of the day.'

'Indeed, I shall do nothing of the sort,' she answered. 'I am going to lead the army to-day to see if we cannot regain some ground, for I had rather die fighting than be driven back like this, so please don't say I mustn't go; besides, the Owl will protect me; he promised to; didn't you, Owl?' and the Owl nodded.

'But they may shoot the Owl with their arrows, and then——'

'But the Owl before now has conquered Merrymineral himself, and he may still do it. Oh, please don't tell me not to go. If you'll only let me go I'll promise to keep near the Prince of India, and he'll protect me, even if the Owl can't.'

'But the Prince of India is always in the thickest of the fight, and you will be in much greater danger if you keep near him.'

'Oh, never mind the danger; do let me go.'

And she begged so hard that Lord Licec had to give in. She put on a breastplate and a sword, but she would not put on a helmet, for she said that it made her head ache, and that no one would know who she was if she covered her face up. So she only wore a gold circlet on her head, as she usually did, and besides this she carried a silver shield with the royal crest on it, and a small lance just like a knight's spear, only not so heavy, and thus mounted on her white horse she rode to the very front of the line of battle, and there she found the Prince of India at the head of his men.

They had already furled their tents and were quite ready to begin the battle as soon as the others were ready.

The Prince was very much astonished when he saw her, for it was the last place in the world he had expected to see her in.

'Do you really mean to say,' he exclaimed, 'that Lord Licec allowed you to come out to the field of battle? Why, he must be mad.'

'Oh no, he's not,' answered the Princess; 'but you see if I only beg hard enough he'll let me do whatever I like, and then I promised to keep near you, for I thought you would protect me. However, you don't seem very glad to see me—perhaps you think I shall hinder you—so I'll go and ask some one else to take care of me, as you don't seem to relish the task.   Good-morning'; and she began to move off; but she knew very well that he would not let her go like that, and to tell the truth she rather hoped he wouldn't, for she thought she would like him to take care of her better than any one else in the army.   Of course he did stop her and said .

'If you really insist on stopping on the field no one is more fit to take care of you than I.   So *do* stop.'

And she allowed herself to be persuaded to stop with him.

Just as they had managed to arrange it so, a trumpet blew in the direction of the town, and immediately troops of knights and men-at-arms began to pour out of the gates, and to form the line of battle, and as each band of men came along they cheered long and loud at the sight of the Princess, and the Princess felt very happy, for she liked to know that her people loved her.   Gradually the immense army came into one long line of

glistening steel, and again the trumpets
sounded, and the line began to move
forward like a wave of the sea as it
runs up the smooth sand sweeping all
before it.   The smooth plain which
was to form the battlefield was dotted
here and there with troops of cattle
which had come down in the night
from the hills to feed on the long sweet
grass, and they raised their heads in
astonishment at the line of knights
and bowmen that marched slowly
down on them; so they shook their
heads and galloped off straight in
front of the line, with their tails high
in the air, and they were in such
blind haste that they charged right
through the lines of the enemy who
were now approaching, and not only
through them they went, but also
through their camp, tossing the tents
into the air with their horns as they
went by.   However, at last they
reached the hills, and did not disturb
the combatants any more.

G

Meanwhile the armies had got quite close together—so close indeed that they could see each other's faces quite plainly—but they did not seem particularly eager to fight. So when they had got thus far they halted, and looked at one another.

As yet Merrymineral had not arrived, for to tell the truth he was never a very early riser, and he did not see why he should hurry himself—for you see he was quite sure of winning the battle without much trouble.

Just opposite the Princess was the flower of the enemy, and she recognised many of the great men of the countries that had rebelled with Merrymineral. They did not seem particularly happy where they were, and especially when the Princess looked at them they looked very red and uncomfortable, as if they did not like it at all.

'I do believe they're ashamed of themselves,' she said to the Prince; and he answered :

'They certainly look like it.'

'Do you think,' she asked, 'if I were to go over to them and offer to pardon them that they would leave Merrymineral and come on my side?'

The Prince thought a moment.

'I believe they would,' he said; 'only if I were you I would not go, I should send an ambassador or a herald.'

But the Princess shook her head.

'That would never do,' she said. 'I'm sure they'd be offended at that. Why, it would look as if I thought they were not to be trusted, and besides they would not hurt me. No, I'll go to them quite alone.'

But the Prince said: ·

'You had better let me go with you, for if they did attack you it would be awkward; besides, you know you promised to keep near me all the morning, and if you go without me you will not be keeping your promise, don't you see?'

So the Princess said:

'Well, I suppose you're right, only you must come alone.'

And as he agreed to this they went forward. Her own army evidently did not understand what she meant to do, nor, for the matter of that, did the enemy, but as they had neither of them received the order to commence fighting they neither of them advanced.

So the Prince and Princess advanced at a gentle trot until they were quite close to the others, and the Owl sat on her shoulder.

When they were quite close the knights tried to get one behind the other just as if they had done something they ought not to have done, and were each afraid of being punished first.

In particular the Princess noted the giant and dwarf, the ambassadors of the evening before; they tried to hide themselves behind the others altogether. For the dwarf this was easy enough, but for the poor giant, he could not manage it at all, he was so very big.

However, she did not look at all angry, and she only said :

'Good-morning, my lords.'

And they replied in chorus :

'Good-morning, your Majesty.'

So she went on :

'I have come to ask you why you have assisted my rebellious subject, and what grievance you have? If there is any I will try to redress it.'

One of the nobles replied :

'We have no grievances.'

'Then why have you fought against me?'

'Because we could not help it, your Majesty.'

'But I should have thought you could have helped fighting.'

'I mean, your Majesty, that Merry-mineral threatened to kill us all if we did not fight.'

'Then you were not very brave. But that has nothing to do with it.

What I wish to know is, whether you will now submit to me again?'

'We would most willingly; only perhaps your Majesty might inflict some punishment on us for our misdeeds.'

But the Princess shook her head.

'No; I will give you all a free pardon if you return to your allegiance.'

So the nobles gave a shout of joy, and they seemed quite happy again. And the Princess too was overjoyed; however, she ordered them to go each knight to his own men and to tell them what had happened, and to conduct them to her own army.

So they all went and did as they were told, and soon the whole army of Merrymineral melted away, with the exception of a very few, and these were mostly the servants of Merrymineral himself, and of the giant and the dwarf, who still remained faithful to him. However they seemed quite unhappy about it.

So the Princess turned to them and said :

'And you, sirs, will you not also join me?'

But the giant shook his head, and the dwarf said snappishly :

'Don't you know we can't?'

But the Princess answered :

'No; I do not know why you can't.'

So the dwarf snarled :

'We're bound to serve him for a certain time, whether we like it or not. ·I'm the King of the Underground Gnomes—we live in tunnels under the earth, and never come up unless we're obliged to.'

And the giant said :

'I'm the Spirit of the Woods— that's why I'm dressed in leaves like this; and I'm the King of the Foresters, and we live in trees.'

But just at this moment a frightful roar came from the camp :

'Why don't you begin?' it came.

It was so sudden that it quite

startled the Princess, but the giant
shook his head mournfully :

'He always roars like that when he's
in a temper. He'll be coming out in
a moment, and won't there be a row?'

Just then the voice came again.

'Bring Popfelwuski to the door.'

'Popfelwuski's his dragon that he
rides on,' said the giant.

And then some servants led the
dragon to the door of one of the
tents.

It was a most marvellous-looking
creature, for it had eyes as large as
tea-trays, and they twinkled awfully;
and it was golden-coloured all over,
and it shone so brightly in the sun
that it made the Princess's eyes quite
ache to look at it. And it was
growling and prancing and kicking up
the dust, and making more fuss than
fifty horses could have done. Just
then the tent opened and Merrymineral
came out. He looked just as usual,
and had not any armour or weapons

except a huge battle-axe, which must have weighed nearly a ton, but he carried it with the greatest ease, although he was an old man—for he was over eight hundred years old. He vaulted on to his dragon's back with very great ease, and putting his spurs to its golden sides made it gallop at a great rate. As yet he had not seen what had happened to his army, for he was rather short-sighted, but when he had got within a few yards of where it ought to have been, he suddenly stopped as if he were bewildered, but then his eye fell on the Princess and he roared out :

'Oh, it's you, is it? I'll soon do for you,' and he made his dragon fly towards the Princess at a very great rate. But precisely the same thing happened now as had happened once before, for the dragon came to a sudden stop as if it had hit against a wall. The Prince of India did not understand it at all.

'Had we not better retreat and join the rest of the army?' he said.

But the Princess answered :

'Oh no, we're quite safe here. He won't be able to get at us. Only you'd better come a little closer to me, because he might be able to hit you.'

So the Prince came a good deal closer, and they sat watching the frantic efforts of Merrymineral to get at them, but it was no use. Suddenly, however, he changed his mode of attack. He made his dragon fly high into the air— so high indeed that it would have been invisible if its golden coat had not shone brightly in the sun. It was quite unpleasant to look at him, for he was so high up that it made them feel dizzy as it shone out against the sky, miles high. Suddenly, however, just as it was directly over them, it seemed to be growing larger.

'I do believe he's going to drop on us from above'; and so he was. The Prince put up his lance that the dragon

might be spiked on it as it fell. But
he might have saved himself the
trouble, for suddenly, when the thing
had fallen to within a few feet of their
heads, it stopped as if it had fallen on
to the roof of a house, and then it
bounced off again like a ball.

But the Princess had shut her eyes,
so she did not see this ; but when she
opened them she saw the dragon and
Merrymineral lying on the grass in a
heap where they had fallen.

But he was soon on his feet again,
and again he tried to charge at the
Princess ; but it was no use, and he
only tired himself. At last the Princess began to get tired too, so she
turned to the Prince and said :

'I think we've had enough of this—
don't you ? '

And he replied :

'Oh, plenty ; but I don't see how
we're to get rid of him, unless I go
out and fight him.'

But the Princess answered :

'Oh, I don't think you need do that, although it's very good of you to offer —but you've forgotten all about the Owl.' So she took the Owl off her shoulder, and putting it on the horse's head with its face to her she asked it:

'You can drive him away, can't you, dear Owl?'

And the Owl nodded gravely. So the Princess said:

'Then I wish you would—only don't hurt him; only drive him away.'

As she said this a wonderful change came over the Owl. It began to grow bigger and bigger, until it quite covered them over as it spread its wings to fly. Merrymineral seemed to know what was coming, for he drew his steed's reins up tight and examined his stirrups and saddle. And then, as the Owl flew towards him, he tried to spur the golden dragon against him; but the dragon refused to move, and at last it turned and bolted with its tail between its legs, like a whipped dog.

Merrymineral tried hard to stop it, but he might as well have tried to stop a mad bull. As he could not stop, and the Owl was catching him up, he turned in his saddle and hurled his heavy battle-axe at the Owl; but the Owl caught it as it flew, and flung it back with such good aim and force that it hit the dragon on the back and cut it clean in half, so that it fell from under Merrymineral and left him standing on the ground.

But when he saw that the Owl was quite close to him, a wonder happened —for he suddenly caught fire at his feet and shot up into the air just as you may have seen a rocket do, and he shot right away, so that the last they saw of him was just as he disappeared over the mountains. But the Owl flew back to its mistress quite small again, and it perched once more on her shoulder as affectionately as ever. As to the golden dragon, it had disappeared altogether—and the funny part was that nothing was heard of it ever after, and no one knew how it had gone—so that the only thing that remained was the battle-axe, and that took seven men to lift it. However, the main thing was that Merrymineral had departed, and there seemed no likelihood of his returning.

So you may imagine how great the Princess's joy was..

As soon as he had quite disappeared, she said :

'That really does seem to be the last of him.'

But the Prince shook his head :

'You never know when that sort of man will turn up again; and in the meantime what are we to do with the giant and the dwarf? I suppose we had better attack them at once and get rid of them.'

'But why?' asked the Princess. 'They don't seem to want to fight much, and why should we attack them ? Let us go and ask them to go away quietly, and I should think they will.'

So they went up to where the giant and the dwarf and their forces were standing.

'What are you going to do now?' she asked of them.

'I don't know,' answered the dwarf, and the giant too shook his head. So the Princess said :

'Will you come and join our rejoicings?'

But the dwarf said :

'No; I must be going back to my kingdom, or I don't know what won't happen.'

And the giant said :

'And I'll go too, or they might rebel there just as your subjects have done.'

So he said good-day, and in three minutes he had disappeared. The dwarf too said good-day quite politely for him, and then he struck the ground with the point of his lance, and immediately the earth opened before him and he marched into the opening at the head of his troops, and with their trumpets blowing and banners waving they disappeared, and the Princess never saw them nor their master again—and to tell the truth she was not very sorry. But the Prince and Princess marched back to the town at the head of the army, and there Lord Licec met them and congratulated the Princess on her success, and the people shouted for joy, and the bells pealed gladly.

So they marched through the town to the principal city, from which you may remember she had set out on the day before. And there they were received with even greater joy, and for six days there was feasting and rejoicing throughout the whole land, but on the seventh day, after the Princess had rewarded the knights who had fought the best, the army dispersed, and the town quieted down, and everything went on just as usual.

Only the Prince of India remained
of all the knights who had fought.
He said he was not well, and wanted
a rest before he set out for India, which
was a long way off. So he stopped
and rested, and the winter changed to
summer, and the summer to autumn,
and he was still there, and he did not
seem as if he were likely to go either.
The time slipped away quietly enough,
and no more was heard of Merrymineral—not even a word. One day
when the Lords of the Council had
finished sitting for the day, and were
departing, Lord Licec remained, as he
always did when he had anything
private to say to the Princess. So
she said :

'Well, my lord, what is it that you
wish to tell to me to-day ? '

'I had come, your Majesty, to make
a suggestion to you that it would be
greatly to the good of the nation if
your Majesty would condescend to
think about marrying some one.'

H

The Princess was so startled that she quite jumped :

'Marry any one ! good gracious me, whom am I to marry ? I don't know any one that I like at all.'

Lord Licec stroked his chin :

'That is rather a drawback,' he said ; 'but I had thought that perhaps the Prince of India might——'

But the Princess interrupted him :

' Oh, he would never do ; besides he would have to ask me, and he won't do that.'

But it might have been noticed that she blushed just a little as she said it, so that perhaps she was not quite sincere in what she said. Lord Licec did not notice that, so he said :

'Well, if he won't suit, the only thing to do is to have a tournament, and then you must marry the winner.'

But she did not seem to like the idea at all.

'Suppose the winner should turn

out a hunchback, or a cripple, or a very hideous man,' she said.

'Your Majesty might arrange it so that the candidates should only be allowed to tilt if they were sufficiently handsome.'

She agreed to the suggestion.

'I suppose it is the only thing to do,' she said; and it was arranged that in four weeks' time a grand tournament was to take place for the hand of the Princess Ismara, and that all the handsome knights in the world could come if they liked.

As to the Owl, when he was asked if he liked the arrangement, he gravely nodded his head; so the Princess felt quite safe in her choice, and the Prince of India felt contented also, for he knew he had a very good chance of winning, unless some knight of whom he had never heard should suddenly turn up. He spent the time in between in practising for the tournament, and he ordered a new set of armour to be sent to him from India in time.

So every one seemed pleased with the arrangement, except, perhaps, the ugly knights, but they kept quiet about it.

The month went away quietly, except that the town was gradually filling with knights, who were coming to take part in the contest. The lists were erected on a plain just outside the town-walls, and on the day before the tournament the free seats were already filled with people, who had come there determined to get places even if they had to wait all day long and had to sleep there all night. As you may imagine, the Princess did not get much sleep that night, for she was naturally in a great fever of excitement thinking about who the knight would be. One thing she was sure about, and that was, that if she did not like him she would not have anything to do with him, even if she had to forfeit her kingdom. However that might be, she did not sleep that night, and on the morrow she felt quite tired. She dressed herself in her most splendid robes, and drove to the lists in a little basket-work pony carriage drawn by eight little mouse-coloured ponies. It was a beautiful day, and the road to the lists was covered with people who were going to look on, or to take part in the tournament, and as she went by they drew up their horses to bow to her, for she had specially forbidden them to cheer — she said it made her head ache. So she drove down the hard, white road bowing and smiling to the people, and they smiled and looked glad too, for they were very fond of their Princess.

After she had gone along thus for about five minutes she overtook the Prince of India, who was going the same way on his famous horse. The Prince did not seem to see her—in fact he was engaged in looking very hard at his spur on the other side.

But the Princess did not mean to pass him like that, so she said cheerfully :

'Good morning, Prince.'

He looked up quite astonished :

'Good morning, your Majesty !' he said, and he took off his cap and bowed low in his saddle, for you see he had not got his armour on—he had sent it on with his page.

The Princess did not know exactly what to say next, so for a moment they were silent, and the Prince trotted quietly by her side.   At last she said :

'Are you, too, going to look on at the tournament ?'

The Prince answered :

'I had purposed taking part in it— that, ahem !—is if your Majesty thinks I am sufficiently handsome, and if you have no other objection.'

The Princess answered quickly :

'Oh, no objection at all. I should like it very much—that is, if you are content to run the risk of your life for such a small prize.'

But the Prince only answered :

'Oh, your Majesty!' and her Majesty flushed a little at his reply.

So they went on again in silence, and the road began to get fuller and fuller of people, and the Princess had her time so taken up by managing her ponies—for she was driving herself, you know—that she could not say much.

However, just as they reached the entry she said :

'By the bye, what seat have you got?'

'I believe they've given me a seat over on the south side,' he answered.

'Dear me, how careless of them. Why, you'll have the sun in your face all the time you're not tilting, and it will give you such a headache. You'd better come into the Royal Box—they've got an awning over that, and you'll be able to see much better. Do come.'

So the Prince gave his horse to his page and went with the Princess and the Owl—for you must remember that the Owl was always perched on her shoulder.

The lists were very gay with horses, and knights, and heralds, and many and great were the knights that intended to tilt. They had come from the uttermost parts of the world—from Kensington, from Nubia, from—well, from everywhere, for you see they did not get the chance of fighting for a princess every day. So you may imagine how many suitors there were. Nearly a thousand came, but a good many of them were not considered handsome enough, so they either went away in a tiff or else they stayed to look on. Still it would take a good three days before the last man had tilted.

The entrance of the Princess was the signal for the music to begin, and the procession of knights filed past,

each one bowing to the Princess and
making his horse perform feats of skill.
And then the tournament began and
the knights charged each other, each
in their turn. The way they managed
it was for each knight to throw lots for
the order of their fighting, and then
they were to be divided into two bodies
—the challengers and those to be
challenged ; and as it came to the turn
of each challenger, he rode out and
touched the shield of the knight on the
other side with whom he wished to fight,
and then the victors were to fight it
out among themselves until they were
all finished except one.

The Prince of India happened to be
one of the challengers, and his turn
did not come until the afternoon. So
during the morning he sat in the Royal
Box talking to the Princess or to the
lords and maids in waiting.

But the Princess did not seem to
enjoy the gentle and joyous passages
of arms at all, for you see she was very

soft-hearted, and did not like to see the
knights knocked off their horses so
very roughly. So, on the whole, she
was not nearly so gáy as the Prince,
and indeed, she seemed very unhappy
when he went to put on his panoply as
his turn came near.

However, he soon afterwards came
into the lists dressed in his full armour,
and you may be sure he looked very
splendid, mounted on his black horse—
for his armour was entirely of silver,
and his shield shone so brightly that it
hurt one's eyes to look at it, and his
long plumes floated in the wind a great
many yards behind him.

The spectators cheered him very
much as he caracoled from one end of
the lists to the other, and the Princess
quite brightened up as she saw him.

'I wonder whose shield he's going
to touch?' she said to herself; and
when she saw who it was she said :

'Good gracious me ! he's challenged
the Knight of Sarragos ; why, he's the

greatest knight in the world. Oh dear, I'm sure the Prince will be beaten.'

However, the knights were now going each to his own station at different ends of the lists. The horses seemed quite as excited as the knights, and they champed their bits and foamed and pawed up the ground, while the heralds read the challenge from the Prince of India to the Knight of Sarragos.

It seemed as if the Princess was right about the strength of the Knight, for he was of enormous size, and he looked a veritable pillar of steel as he sat on his horse listening to the challenge. However, the trumpets for the charge sounded, and away went the knights straight towards each other like arrows, each one looking along his spear to see that it was aimed truly for his adversary —covering himself well with his shield. They went so fast that they could hardly be seen, and the crash when they met was louder than the loudest peal of thunder you ever heard.

The Princess shut her eyes at the sound. But she could not keep them shut, for the people were cheering very loudly. So she opened them reluctantly, and she seemed quite glad to see that the Knight of Sarragos had been thrown from his horse by the shock and was rolling in the dust. It was rather odd that she should be pleased at this, because as a rule she was sorry for the conquered knight ; for myself I rather think she had wanted the Prince to win all along. Anyhow she congratulated him warmly on his success when he came back to his seat, and for the rest of the day she did not seem much interested in the tilting although some of it was very good, too.

So the first two days passed away and nothing particular happened. The Prince of India took his turn with the rest, till at last the third day came and there were only ten knights left. These, too, the Prince overcame, and it seemed as if all was over and he had gained the prize ; but while the heralds were still calling for any one to come and defeat the Prince, and while every one was holding their breath in expectation, a loud blast from a trumpet sounded through the air, and at the other end of the lists a knight appeared. He was a very tall and splendid-looking knight—for his armour was of gold, and the crest on his helmet-top was a dragon carved out of a rose-red ruby of enormous size ; and the point of his lance was made of one diamond, that sparkled in the sun a great deal more brightly than any dewdrop on a spring morning. And as to handsome, why he was a perfect blaze of handsome-ness, so that there could be no objection to him. The only thing was, no one knew who he was, or where he came from.

So the Princess beckoned him to

her, and he came and bowed low in his saddle.

'Who are you, Sir Knight?' she asked; 'and where do you come from?'

'I am the Knight of London, your Majesty.'

'London, London; where's that?— I've never heard of it.'

'London is the capital city of England.'

'But where *is* England?' she asked.

'I had thought that every one had heard of England,' he said. 'However, as no report of England has ever reached your ears, I will tell your Majesty. The British Islands, of which England is one, are a set of small islands off the west coast of Europe. They are composed of England, Scot——'

But here the Princess interrupted him.

'I thank you, Sir Knight, for your information, but just now the tournament is waiting for you, and I am not very fond of geography lessons.'

The Knight bowed again, and retired to take up his place in the lists.

'How very handsome he is!' said the Princess to one of her maids in waiting.

And the lady answered:

'Oh, quite too handsome!'

However, by this time both the knights were in their places, and the Princess nodded to the heralds to give the signal.

'*Laissez aller,*' they cried, which is the French for 'Go.'

And they did go with a vengeance—they went so fast that they looked all blurred together like streaks of lightning. And when they met, it was louder than thunder, louder than the shock of avalanches, louder than—well, louder than everything you ever heard, except perhaps when some one lets the tea-tray fall down the kitchen stairs.

And when the dust cleared up, the poor Knight of India was rolling on the ground in a heap, composed of himself and his horse. But the Princess did not seem very sorry for him—so wags the world.

The Knight of London, however, was seated in his saddle as firmly as if he were part of it; and as there seemed nothing else to do, he commanded his heralds to challenge any one who should wish to dispute his right to the victory. But no one came out, for either there was no one else left, or else the knights were afraid to enter the lists against one who had overthrown so easily so doughty a knight as the Prince of India. However that might be, no one turned up, so the Knight of London was declared the victor. The shout that was raised at this declaration was not very tremendous, for most of the people liked the Prince of India, whereas they did not care much for the new-comer. But he did not seem to mind it much, and he went smilingly to the Princess. As he came before the royal presence he made his horse kneel, and advance kneeling, till he was quite close.

Then he said:

'As no one appears to dispute my right I believe I am the victor, and in virtue of that right I claim your Majesty's hand.'

But the Princess laughed.

'Oh, we'll see about that to-morrow; there'll be plenty of time then. Meanwhile, this evening we are going to give a ball at the palace, to which all who have taken part in the tournament are invited. Of course you'll come, won't you?'

'Of course I will, at your invitation, your Majesty, but——'

What he was going to say was drowned in an immoderate fit of laughter, which came from the Prince of India.

'Ha! ha! ha!' he laughed. 'Can't you see who it is you're talking too?' he continued, talking to the Princess.

I

The Princess drew herself up.

'I believe I am talking to the Knight of London,' she said severely.

'The Knight of London! why he's no more the Knight of London than I am. Why, your Majesty must be blind or mad, or both, not to see who he is. Blind's not enough to express it. You——'

But he got no farther, for the Princess called for the police to arrest him, but before they could get at him he had fainted; for the spear of the Knight of London had gone right through his side. So the Princess told the police to lift him up gently and to carry him to his house in the town.

But the Knight of London frowned:

'If I were you, your Majesty, I should order them to cut his head off on the first opportunity. To call you mad and blind—why I've never heard of such a thing.'

But the Princess said:

'That would never do. Why, he is an independent prince, and if I hurt him it would bring on a war with India, and goodness knows what else. However, I'll have him turned out of the kingdom as soon as he is well enough to go. However, I am going back now. Mind and be in time this evening.'

So he went to doff his armour, and she drove home once more—this time without the poor Prince, who was being carried behind in an ambulance waggon. The rest of the day passed off somehow, and the night came at last, as nights are in the habit of doing, and with the night came knights—no longer dressed in steel armour, but gorgeous in velvet and silk and evening dress. But, however gorgeous and fine they might be, the Knight of London outstripped them all, in dress, manners, looks, and everything else, and the Princess said he had the best step of any one she had ever known—and she ought to know, for she danced with him a great many times. In fact, by the end of the ball she had forgotten all about the poor Prince, for the Knight of London was a most enchanting person —although one thing did seem strange, and that was, that the Knight seemed positively afraid of the Owl; and at supper-time he actually refused to sit on the right hand of the Princess because the Owl was sitting on her right shoulder.

But the Owl took no notice of him at all, and never even looked at him, so she thought it was only a rather foolish prejudice on his part. However, the ball came to an end at last, and the Princess went to bed and dreamt pleasantly of some one, but it was not the Prince this time.

And the Prince lay tossing on his bed only half dreaming, and not pleasantly, of some one, and it *was* the Princess. As for the Knight of London, nobody knows what he dreamt about; and, to tell the truth, nobody cared. But the Owl sat at the head of the Princess's bed, and slept calmly, — he did not dream ; owls are not in the habit of dreaming —they are a good deal wiser.

When the next morning came, the Knight of London came with it, and he wanted to know when the Princess would marry him; but the Princess put him off — for somehow, although she liked him very much, she did not altogether relish the idea of marrying so soon. So she told him that he must wait until the Lords of the Council had given their consent, and they were not going to meet till the next day, so he would have to wait till then. But the Knight did not like this at all.

' At all events, my dear Princess,' he said, 'you might promise to marry me, for, after all, I did win the tournament, you see, and so——'

But the Princess put her hand to her chin and rubbed it softly as if she were thinking very deeply—and no doubt she was—and shook her head emphatically.

'No; I can't promise until the Council have given their consent, for you see that would be unconstitutional, and I can't be that even for you.'

The Knight seemed quite angry.

'Bother the unconstitutionality,' he said; 'what does the stupid old Council want to blunder into such matters?'

But the Princess stopped him:

'Oh, you mustn't say that—please don't say that,' she said; 'it's not a stupid old Council, it's a very nice old Council, and it's much nicer than you are. When you get angry like that you're not at all nice—so just be quiet; now do.'

And he had to be quiet, for he was afraid of making her really angry.

She too was afraid she had hurt his feelings by telling him to be quiet. So she asked him to join the hunt that was preparing outside, and he of course

accepted her invitation, for you see
he was only too glad to make it up.
They rode out of the town, and soon
a deer was started, and the chase swept
through the tall trees after it over the
thick carpet of fallen leaves and
between the trunks of the beech-trees.
As a rule the Princess's horse was
swifter than any of the deer they
started, but this one seemed an exception to the rule, for it went on at just
the rate she did, keeping always
at the same speed whether she pulled
her horse in or let it go at the
top of its speed. The Princess was
quite annoyed at this. Gradually she
passed all the knights and huntsmen
who were labouring forward at full
gallop, and then she came up with the
hoarse - tongued hounds, who were
running steadily along with their noses
close to the ground. And then she
passed them too, and their deep
mouthing sounded behind, and gradually the shouts of the huntsmen and

the cries of the dogs and all the sounds of the chase died away behind, and still the deer kept steadily forward. Just at this time she noticed the heavy gallop of a horse behind her, and looking round she saw the Knight of London cantering easily behind. So she slackened her speed a little to let him come up, and then she stopped to let the rest of the chase come up with her; and when she stopped the deer stopped too, and nibbled quietly at a flower that was growing at the foot of a tree.

By this time the Knight had come up with her, and she said:

'So here you are. What an annoying thing that deer is—I can't catch it up, do whatever I may, and my horse used to be thought the fastest in the world, except one,' she added, after a moment.

'That is strange,' said the Knight. 'I used always to think mine the fastest in the world, and indeed, your

Majesty, I think it is quite as fast as yours.'

'I do believe it is,' she said. 'It's most annoying; every second person I see now has a horse as fast as mine. However, we'll try a race as soon as the rest have caught us up.'

Just at that moment a hound's bay came from close behind them, and the deer started off again.

'There it goes,' said the Princess; and again she started off, and the Knight kept close beside her. They went faster than ever, and she could hardly breathe because of the wind, but the Knight kept steadily by her side, and would not be out-distanced. Just at this moment she happened to look upwards, and there was the Owl sailing quietly along just over her head, flapping his wings lazily as if there were no need for exertion, although they were going at such a rate that the Princess could hardly keep her eyes open—just as when you put your head out of the window of a railway train that is going pretty fast—a thing, by the bye, that it is to be hoped you never do, or you might get your nose chopped off against a post. When she looked down from the Owl, to her surprise the deer had vanished altogether, and although she rubbed her eyes she could not see it anywhere; and although they galloped still farther on, no deer made its appearance, and the forest had become dark and thick and she had never been there before. So she drew her horse in so suddenly that its hoofs threw up the copper-coloured beech-leaves in showers, and the Knight shot some distance in advance. However, he turned and came back. So the Princess said :

'What are we to do now?'

'Go back, I suppose,' he answered.

'But I don't know the way,' she said, 'and we are near the country of the Magi, and they're the most frightful creatures, who would tear us up and eat us if they knew where to find us.'

The Knight smiled :

'I could save you from them,' he said.

But the Princess said reflectively :

'I don't know so much about that, for you see they're very strong—and how dark it's getting; it must be past five, and it will soon be night.'

I daresay if she had been alone she would have had a good cry, but that wouldn't do before strangers.

It was still getting darker and she began to feel very uncomfortable, for the howl of a wolf came down on the breeze, and a squirrel that had been searching for nuts darted home to its hole, scuttling along as fast as it could.

So she said :

'Come, let us be quick and get away.'

'Promise to marry me first.'

But she only said :

'Oh, I'll see about that when we're safe—so do come.'

What the Knight would have answered was never known, for just then the Owl, who was seated on her shoulder, gave a mournful 'Tu-whoo,' at which the horse of the Knight jumped back nearly ten feet and almost threw him with the unexpected shock. But before she could do anything a hunter burst from the bushes near at hand and said :

'Hurry, Princess, hurry ; the Magi have heard of your whereabouts, and they are coming at full speed here. Come, be quick.'

But the Princess said :

'But what will you do, old man ? for you have no horse.'

But he smiled contemptuously.

'Horse ! I don't want a horse—why, I can run as well as any deer. Come, come.'

And he caught the bridle of her horse and away they went, and for the moment she forgot all about the Knight, for from behind came the sound of crashing branches, and she knew that the Magi were following them. But the old hunter ran in front of the horse, tugging at the bridle-rein, and shouting to her to go faster, so she leant forward and whispered in her horse's ear, and it stretched forward with such speed that it outsped the wind. Gradually the sounds behind began to get less and less, and the wood began to get lighter, and at last they jumped a little brook, and were at the end of the forest in a smooth meadow. Here the old man stopped.

'You are safe now,' he said. And she drew a sigh of relief.

'At last!' she said; 'but how can I reward you, my preserver? Would you like a lock of my hair, or a purse full of gold, or a—— ? well that wouldn't do—you see I can't well offer to marry you, though that's what princesses generally do to their preservers. You'd better choose something for yourself. I will grant it, whatever it is.'

But the old man shook his head.

'I want no reward, your Majesty; I only did my duty. I couldn't have done less. See, here come some of the hunters whom you left behind.'

And just then several of them came up, and when they saw her they shouted and blew their horns to let the others know that the Princess was found. But the huntsman said:

'Good-day, your Majesty. I must go.'

'But you haven't got your reward yet.'

But he shook his head.

'I want no reward,' he said; and before the Princess could say any more he stepped into the forest and was seen no more; so she turned her horse towards the town.

On her way she met the head huntsman, so she drew rein and said:

'Why did you not follow on the scent of the deer?'

'It lay so thinly, your Majesty, that the dogs could not follow, and they soon gave in.'

'But you should have followed me, at any rate.'

'Ah, your Majesty, we might as well have tried to prove the moon was made of green cheese. Besides, your Majesty had one cavalier; and sometimes two's company and three's none.'

Just at this moment the Princess remembered the Knight.

'Good gracious!' she said, 'what has become of the Knight—have none of you seen him?'

But none of them had, and although the question went far and wide no news came of him, nor could he be seen anywhere.

'He must have been caught by the Magi—if so, he will have been devoured to a certainty! Poor Knight!'

The chief huntsman seemed excited:

'Your Majesty has not been near the country of the Magi surely?' he said.

'I was almost too near, and the poor Knight has probably been torn to pieces in trying to drive them back.'

'Your Majesty should be thankful that knights are so faithful,' said the chief huntsman; 'but perhaps, after all, he has escaped by a different path.'

But the Princess sighed:

'I am afraid not,' she said

However, she rode on to the town to consult Lord Licec as to what had better be done. But when she got there she found that he was out of town and would not be back till next morning. So the poor Princess had to go back home and wait—but she looked so pale that her ladies-in-waiting insisted on sending for the doctor. He came in a hurry, and asked her of course what was the matter, and when she told him he shook his head.

'I'm afraid he's got rather a poor chance, for these Magi haven't had a good meal of one of your Majesty's subjects for nearly three weeks, and they were uncommonly hungry. But if your Majesty will allow me to feel your pulse, I——'

So she gave him her hand, and he took out his watch and began to count. 'One, two, three, four'; but just then he looked up and saw the Owl sitting on the Princess's shoulder, and his hand trembled so much that he dropped his watch, and it smashed to atoms on the floor.

'Oh dear, there goes ten and six-pence,' he groaned; 'and I shan't be able to get another for ever so long. D'you know, your Majesty, I think you are somewhat feverish; and you had better go to bed. And meanwhile, the Owl is too exciting for you; if you could let it be put in a cellar and

K

let it have nothing to eat for, say, three weeks, perhaps it might not be so fiery after that.'

The Princess smiled:

'Perhaps you would like to take him there yourself,' she said.

But the doctor said:

'Good gracious! no. I think he's perfectly capable of taking himself without any assistance. D'you know, your Majesty, I've got a very pressing case outside; and if you will excuse me I will retire.'

And he retired so quickly that he left his umbrella behind him—for you see he was very frightened of the Owl.

Acting on his advice the Princess went to bed, and dismissed her ladies-in-waiting and told them not to come to the room again until she called for them.

And then she lay with her hand under her head thinking of nothing in particular, and the Owl sat on the top of the canopy over her bed.

Suddenly she heaved a deep sigh.

'I wish I knew what had become of him,' she thought to herself.

'You wouldn't like it if you did know,' said a strange cracked voice that seemed to come from nowhere in particular. She started up and looked all round the room, but there was no one to be seen; so she thought it was all imagination, and lay down again. And again she thought to herself, 'How I should like to be with him.'

'No, you wouldn't,' said the voice.

This time she was sure it came from the Owl, so she asked quite softly, 'Did you say that, cherished Owl?'

And the Owl answered:

'I did.'

'But I thought you could not speak, dear Owl.'

'Well, you see, I can sometimes— when it's necessary.'

'But how did you know what I was thinking?—for I did not speak aloud.'

'Ah! you see, Princess, I can't tell
you that—it's quite enough for you
that I can tell.'

'But why do you say I should not
like to see him?'

'Because you wouldn't.'

'Why? Is he all torn to pieces by
the Magi?'

'Torn to pieces!—not he,' laughed
the Owl.

'Oh! that is good news,' said she
quite joyfully. 'Oh! do take me to
him, dear Owl.'

'Very well, Princess. But I warn
you, you won't be pleased with what
you see.' But the Princess was quite
confident.

'Oh yes, I shall, dear Owl—when
shall we go?'

'At once, if you like—the sooner
the better.'

'Oh! you dear Owl. I'll go and
get dressed at once.'

So she ran into her dressing-room
and dressed herself in no time, without

bothering to call up any of her ladies-in-waiting about it. Then she went back to the room where the Owl was waiting for her.

He was sitting on the floor near the fire, blinking quietly at the coals, and he did not at first notice her entry, so she said :

'Well, good Owl, shall I send for the horse?'

'What for?' asked the Owl.

'To ride on, I suppose!' she answered.

'Oh, that's it, is it? That would never do. Just get on my back, and I'll see if I can't carry you somewhat faster than a horse could.'

So she got on his back, although she was rather afraid she would crush him altogether. But somehow, when she sat down, she sank deep into his warm feathers,—either she had grown small, or the Owl had grown very big all of a sudden. Without the least shock they passed through the wall, and out into the clear star light.

'Good Owl,' said the Princess, 'you won't let me fall, will you?' for, to tell the truth, she felt rather afraid on the whole; but the Owl answered:

'No, of course not; you're quite safe, only you'd better keep close to me, for we shall go pretty fast, and the wind will be sharp enough to cut your hair off.'

So she sat still, protected against the wind, and looking at the twinkling stars—for the Owl flew so high that he almost rubbed some of them out of their places.

The wind whistled loud in the wings of the Owl, but his flight was so regular that she almost fell asleep, and was quite happy—for you see she felt quite safe. Presently the straight flight of the Owl changed, and he began to circle round and round, and then they dropped quickly towards the earth, and the Owl stopped.

'You can get off now,' he said, and she stepped off his back.

'Take care,' he said next; and she rubbed her eyes in astonishment, for she found herself on the top of a roof.

'I told you you wouldn't like it if you came,' he said. 'But you'd better look down below if you want to see anything that's going on,' and he gravely seated himself on her shoulder, for he seemed quite small again. So the Princess looked down, and she saw at some distance below a large fire that was blazing in a sort of courtyard, and then she saw that it was the battlements of a castle on which they were standing. Presently a horrible-looking old witch came within the glow of the fire—she was an awful old creature too, and she almost made the Princess cry out from fright. She seated herself near the fire, and began to beat the ground angrily with the handle of a broom that she carried, and every now and then muttered as she did so :

'How awfully late he is. Why don't he come?' and various other complaints of his lateness.

'But who is he?' asked the Princess of the Owl in a whisper.

'Wait, and you'll see,' said the Owl.

Just then something peculiar happened down below—a couple of men appeared suddenly. They did not seem to come from anywhere in particular, but they were there all the same. The Princess almost screamed with astonishment, but she checked herself in time by stuffing a pocket-handkerchief into her mouth, for one of the men whom she saw was the Knight of London, and the other was Magog the King of the Magi; and the Knight of London did not seem to be on bad terms with the King of the Magi.

'You've come at last,' growled the

old woman, in a voice something between the squeaking of a slate-pencil on a slate and the growling of a bear with a sore head.

'I couldn't come any sooner, mother,' said the Knight of London soothingly; 'you see I had to wait for her to promise to marry me.'

'Well, has she promised?' said the witch.

'Not yet.'

'Then why on earth not?'

'She said she had to wait for the consent of the Council.'

'Why didn't you eat her?' said Magog sleepily; and then, without waiting for an answer, he curled himself up close to the fire and went to sleep.

But the old witch went on:

'Well, and what are your plans now?'

'I'm going back to-morrow morning, and I'm going to take old Magog and pretend that he's my prisoner of war, and then the stupid old Council will say I've done a service to the State, and they will give me the hand of the Princess for my pains.'

'But supposing they don't?'

'Then I shall cut them all to pieces, and kill the Princess, and make myself king by force—for you see nothing can cut through my armour, except one thing.'

'And what's that?' asked the witch.

'Well, I don't mind telling you, mother, because you won't go and tell any one—it's *Paper*!'

'That's a funny sort of thing to cut through armour.'

'It may be funny,' answered the Knight, 'but it's true all the same, and if the Prince of India had found it out I should not be where I am now; only he didn't, you see.'

'So much the worse for him,' said the witch; 'but is there nothing at all but paper that can cut through it?'

'Well, there is one thing that can—
the beak of the Owl, to wit.'

'Tu - whoo!' suddenly cried the
Owl.

The effect of this sudden cry was
tremendous. The Knight clung to his
mother, and cried out in a piteous
voice :

'Oh, mother! mother! it's the Owl;
save me!'

'How on earth can I save you if
you hang on me like this?' said his
mother. 'Just throw some more wood
on, so that we can see this Owl, and
I'll fling my broom at it, and see if
that won't bring it down.'

But the Princess leant her head to
the Owl, and said :

'Dear Owl, let's go. I've seen
quite enough.'

And the Owl seemed to think the
same, for he said :

'All right. Just get on my back
again, and we'll go.'

So she did as she was told, and no

sooner had she got on his back than she fell asleep, and remembered no more until she found herself lying on her bed with the early morning sun shining through the lattice.

She rubbed her eyes in astonishment, and it seemed as if it had been all a dream. But it all was so clear on her mind, and besides she had on her riding-clothes just as she had put them on to go with the Owl.

To make herself feel more sure she said to the Owl:

'Good Owl, was it a dream?'

And the Owl shook his head, but although she asked him several times to speak she could not get the least word out of him, although he always shook his head if she asked him if it was a dream.

Just then a tremendous noise in the street made her run to the window, and there she saw the Knight of London coming up to the door, dragging the King of the Magi behind him in chains, and the people of the town were following him in an excited crowd, which caused all the noise, for they were naturally very glad to see their old enemy in chains.

The Knight rode straight up to the palace door, and when he saw the Princess at the window he smiled and said :

'Good morning, your Majesty—you see I am returned.'

And the Princess said ;

'Good morning,' as if she were very glad to see him, for she had not yet quite made up her mind about what she was going to do—for of course she could not marry him after what she had seen the night before. So she drew back from the window to think about it—for it would never do to try to get rid of him by force. At last she hit upon a plan—she had to think of it herself—for the Owl would tell her nothing.

She went to the door of her room,

but there were no guards at the door
—they had run down to see what the
shouting was about. But just then
the doctor came up the stairs:

'Good morning, your Majesty,' he
said; 'have you had a good night?'

'A very good night, thank you,
doctor. But that doesn't matter just
now. I want the Prince of India.'

'I beg your pardon,' said the doctor.

'I say I want the Prince of India.'

'The *who*?' said the astonished
doctor.

'The Prince of India.'

'Then I am afraid he can't come.
But if the Knight of London would
do——'

'But he won't! I want the Prince
of India at once.'

'I fear your Majesty can't have him
at once. You *wouldn't* have him once,
you know.'

'But why not?'

'Because at the present moment he
isn't well enough to move.'

'Oh, good gracious!—but why is that?'

'Well, your Majesty, if you'd been thrown from your horse with great violence, and had half a foot of spear stuck into you, besides being mortified at your overthrow, perhaps you would be rather unwell.'

'Oh, poor fellow, I didn't know he was so bad as that. I'll go and see him at once.'

'I think your Majesty had better not.'

'Why not?'

'Because it might excite him too much, and besides, what would the Knight of London——'

But the Princess drew herself up and said:

'I beg your pardon, but I must ask you not to mention that gentleman's name, if you please.'

'Whe—ew,' ejaculated the doctor; 'what's in the wind now?'

'I beg your pardon?' said the Princess.

'I—I only said—it's an east wind now, your Majesty.'

Just then a page came running up, and said that the Knight of London wished to speak to the Princess.

'Tell him that I am not quite well enough to see him now, but I will send a message to him, if he will stop a moment. And on your way just ask Lord Licec to come to me, please.'

'Yes, your Majesty,' said the page, and he disappeared.

In a moment Lord Licec came.

'You sent for me, your Majesty, I believe?'

'I did, my lord. It was about this Knight of London. I have discovered that he is not what he pretends to be at all, for he is in league with the Magi; and this Magog whom he pretends is his prisoner is really nothing of the sort. He is one of his allies, and they are going to break out and kill me, and every one else,

and make themselves masters of everything.'

'Oh, my wig!' suddenly said the
doctor, 'I hope your Majesty won't
let them; if you intend to I shall
depart without delay, for I don't want
to be eaten by this Magog.'

'That's just what I wanted to
prevent by begging the Prince of
India to help us; only you said that
I mayn't see him, doctor.'

'Oh! on the contrary, your Majesty,
it would be the best thing in the world
—we'll go at once.'

'Wait a moment,' said the Princess,
and turning to Lord Licec she went on :

'Now I want you to tell him that
the Lords of the Council say that the
last tournament was unfair, because he
came in fresh at the end. And that
if he wants to—to claim his rights, he
must submit to go through another
tournament. Of course he will—
because he's quite sure of winning—
but he won't this time.'

'Are you quite sure, your Majesty?'

'Oh! quite.   And as all the knights who tilted last time are still in the town, let it take place to-morrow.'

'Yes, your Majesty.'

'And if you could keep him out of the way for a few hours—so that he won't know what I'm going to do—so much the better.'

'I'll challenge him to a game of "Beggar-my-Neighbour"—that generally lasts for a pretty good time.'

'That will do; the longer the better. Now I'm ready, doctor, if you'll conduct me to the Prince.'

So they went out at a back door for fear the Knight of London should see them, and they soon reached the house of the Prince.

At the door was a servant, and they asked him where the Prince was.

'In the garden, your Majesty.   I will go and announce your arrival to him.'

But the Princess said :

'Oh no! never mind—you needn't trouble.'

And they went through into the garden. On the way the Princess said to the doctor:

'I thought you said he was not well enough to get up?'

'I did, your Majesty, but he insisted that he must get up, and be off to India this afternoon, and he was excessively violent when I told him he had better not get up—in fact he—he kicked me downstairs; and if your Majesty has no present need of me I will retire, for to tell the truth he threatened to have me ducked in a horsepond if I came near him again—and he meant it too.'

So the Princess gave him leave to go—in fact she was rather glad he had gone; and she went on walking down the path. It was one of those old-fashioned manor-gardens, full of tall stiff hollyhocks, and damask roses, and beds of thyme and mint, over which

the bees were humming so loudly that
they could be heard over the whole
garden.   As the Princess could not
see him down one path, she turned
into another alley of stiff holly bushes,
but he was not to be seen down there
either ; however, she walked fast to the
end of it—for you see she was rather
impatient.   Now it happened that just
as she turned the corner, the Prince
happened to be coming round too, and
the result was that as they were going
rather fast, and the Prince was the
heavier of the two, the Princess was
thrown back with violence against the
hedge, and she couldn't help ex-
claiming :

'Oh!'—for you see he had trodden
on her toe.   As for the Prince, he could
scarcely stand—for the shock and the
sight of the Princess together produced
a tremendous effect, as you may
imagine—for she was the last person
he had expected to see.

'My goodness !' he said, as soon as

he was able to speak. 'Your Majesty—
I hope I haven't hurt you—I am really
very sorry. I am very sorry—will you
allow me to help you to a seat?
—for I see I have trodden on your
foot.'

Her Majesty said :

'Oh no ! not at all, thank you.'

But all the same she let him give her
his arm, and help her to a seat. It was
a rustic seat—one of those queer seats
made of branches of trees, and it stood
in an arbour formed of rose-bushes, and
there was plenty of room for two ; so
she said :

'Won't you sit down, Prince ?'

But he answered :

'I really have not the time, your
Majesty. I was just about to start for
India, and if your Majesty has no
further need of me I will go, and send
an attendant.'

But she did not seem to hear the last
part of his sentence, for she answered :

'You were going away without saying good-bye to me. Perhaps, however, you intended to call as you passed the palace.'

'I really had not intended to, your Majesty, for you seemed to have so many affairs that I might have interrupted, that I thought it as well to go without troubling you.'

'You shouldn't have thought that. You see I have had so many affairs of State occupying me that I could not possibly get round to call, and you didn't choose to come and see me, which was rather, I think—however, that doesn't matter now. I have come to ask you to stop a little longer—till the day after to-morrow, if you won't stop after that.'

But the Prince shook his head:

'I have to go immediately; affairs of State, you know, demand my presence in India, and I must go at once, your Majesty.'

'Can't you really stop a little Prince?'

' I really can't, your Majesty—that
is——'

'Oh, please do; I'll tell you something, if you like.   I've found out who
the Knight of London is.'

'And then, your Majesty?' inquired
the Prince.

'I don't know what else.   I—I
thought that would be enough for you.'

'I don't understand you, your
Majesty.'

' I mean that when I didn't know he
was a wizard I thought he was very
enchanting; but when I found out he
was an enchanter, I thought you were
enchanter—I mean more enchanting.'

The Prince was just saying :

'Oh, your Majesty,' when a peculiar
noise from the back of the arbour
made them both start, and the Princess
jumped up so violently that the Owl,
who had meanwhile gone to sleep, was
nearly shaken off her shoulder.

'What was that?' she said.

'It sounded like somebody laughing,

or trying to keep from laughing rather.
Just wait a moment, I'll see who it was.'

And he went round behind the
arbour. He soon returned bringing
the doctor with him, and the doctor
did not seem at all happy either.

'Why,' said the Princess, 'I thought
you were going to leave me. How is
it that you came like this behind the
arbour?'

'I might just as well ask your
Majesty why you came here.'

'You might, but it would not be
answering my question.'

'I happened to come round there,
your Majesty, to read a book in the
shade, and I happened to drop off to
sleep, and the noise you heard was my
snoring.'

'But how did you know we heard a
noise if you were asleep at the time?'

'I—eh—I don't exactly know, your
Majesty.'

'It's quite clear you were listening.
I'll excuse you this time, but if I catch

you eavesdropping again I'll make the
Owl take you up into the sky and drop
you—that may be a drop too much for
you. You can go now, but don't do so
any more.'

But the Prince had still hold of
him.

'By the bye,' he said, 'there's a
horsepond near here; I think I'll just
take you there and throw you in,
as I said I would if I caught you
again.'

But the Princess said:

'Oh, let him go, Prince,' and the
doctor hurried off at a great rate.

'I don't think he'll come back again
in a hurry,' said the Prince; 'meanwhile,
what about the Knight of London?'

'I must get rid of him as soon as I
can, and I want you to help me.'

'I, your Majesty—but how?'

'The Council have decided that last
tournament was not fair, because the
Knight came in fresh and you were
already tired out, so they have decided

to have it over again, and you are requested to come and fight—for me.'

'But what is the use of that? he'll
knock me over just as he did before.'

'Oh no! he won't, because I've found
out his secret.' And she told him
about the paper.

At the end the Prince said :

'Oh! that's all right then. I'll be
there, your Majesty.'

'But are you strong enough, do you
think ?'

'Oh yes, your Majesty.'

'And the affairs of State can be put
off till the day after to-morrow. I
promise to let you go as soon as
you have got rid of the Knight for
me.'

'Oh, for the matter of that, there is
no such great hurry. I really needn't
go for some time.'

'But you can go whenever you like,
you know.'

'Thank you, your Majesty.'

'But—a—I don't want you to go,

you know.   In fact I should like you to stop, very much.'

' Then I'll stop as long as you like, your Majesty—for ever, if you like, your Majesty.'

' I should like it very much, Prince,' she answered.

I don't exactly know what happened after that—perhaps you can guess— but they do say that the Owl, who chanced to wake at that moment, positively blushed ; but then people are fond of exaggerating, and the Owl did not seem to object, so I suppose it was all right ; and when the Princess went back to the palace, the Prince was quite good-tempered again, whereas before her visit he had been so angry that all his servants had left in a body— however, they came back when they found he was quiet again.

So the Princess was quite happy once more, as you may imagine, only there was one nasty thing she had to do, and that was to send a note to the

Knight of London thanking him for having taken prisoner the King of the Magi, and hoping that he would be successful at the tournament on the next day—for you see she was not well enough to see him, and he was quite sure of winning, as he had done before, so he did not mind it very much.

The next day came, and the Princess was at the lists as before, and the crowd was just as great too, only there were very many less knights to fight, for the Knight of London was the challenger, and he—well, they had seen how he had treated the Prince of India, and they did not care to be tumbled over in such a very unceremonious way. However, two or three of the bravest in the world came and answered his challenge, but it was no use; they might just as well not have tried, for they were thrown from their horses so violently that they were most of them seriously hurt. So it seemed as if he was going to have it all his own way, for the Prince had as yet not put in an appearance, and the spectators began to call for him—for, as I said before, they liked the Prince better than the Knight; although he was so very handsome, still there was a something about him that they did not like at all. But the Knight had overcome all who had chosen to come against him, and his trumpets were sounding the challenge for the last time, and then their echoes died away and still no answering trumpet came, and the Princess was beginning to feel afraid that he had gone off to India and left her. But just as the Knight was advancing to claim his rights, a trumpet blast rang out brazen and shrill on the still air, and the Prince of India rode into the lists. He was still pale from his illness, but the people cheered him loudly, and the Princess gave a sigh of relief, and quite flushed with joy and excitement.

'He'll win this time,' she said to Lord Licec, who was standing near her.

'I don't know so much about that,' he answered, 'for you see the Knight of London is in very good form to-day; and just look at the Prince's shield — it's made of cardboard, I should think—yes, it is. Ah—I am afraid his last defeat has rather turned his head.'

The Princess smiled and nodded. Lord Licec thought she was nodding to him, but she wasn't; both the smile and the nod were meant for quite another person.

However, the combatants were already in their places, so she signed to the heralds to give the signal.

'*Laissez aller*,' they cried, and once again the Knight and Prince charged each other. This time they did not go so fast, and the spectators could see what took place. It was soon over. The spear of each of the combatants hit exactly the centre of the other's shield. But the spear of the Knight broke as if it had been made of a bulrush. It was not so with the Prince—for his spear pierced through and through the seven-fold shield of the Knight, and the Knight himself was thrown right off his horse on to the ground. He, however, was on his feet in an instant, and rushed at the Prince, who leapt off his horse and confronted the Knight.

The Knight made a pass at the Prince with his rapier, but the Prince caught the thrust on his shield, and the sword came to the same end as the spear. The Knight had still his heavy battle-axe, and he lifted it on high to swing it down on to the head of his opponent. The Prince made no movement to defend himself, and the axe came full on his crest—through the crest it hit its way, and through the steel helmet, but when it got past the steel it hit on a paper helm below, and the axe shivered at the touch as if it had been glass. Then the Prince caught the Knight by the wrist:

'Keep still,' he said, 'or I run you to the heart with my paper dagger.'

'You can't,' sneered the Knight.

'Why not?'

'Because I'm heartless; so you can't hurt my heart.'

The Prince took no notice of what he said. He had turned to the Princess, who was clapping her hands for joy—which was rather an unprincess-like act; but she couldn't help it.

'What shall I do with him?' he said.

'Let him go, I suppose.'

And the Knight was beginning to walk off as fast as he could. But a loud and commanding voice came from behind the Princess, and she looked behind her suddenly, and she almost fainted, for a marvellous change had come over the Owl, and it was still changing. She rubbed her eyes in astonishment, and all the people who could see him did so too, and then a great shout went up from all of 'God save the King!' for it was no longer the Owl they saw—it was the old King.

'Stop!' he cried loudly to the Knight, who was slinking off—'you have not received your reward yet. Just wait a moment, and to prevent mistakes just take your ordinary form.'

And again every one present rubbed their eyes in astonishment—for the handsome calm face of the Knight was shrivelling up, and his raven hair had become an ugly gray, and the people recognised him too as an old acquaintance, for he was—who do you think now? Why, he was Merry-mineral—it seemed as if that day gave two instances of old friends with new faces.

Although he didn't at all seem to want to stay, he was obliged to stop at the King's voice. So he stood in the middle of the lists looking very un-comfortable—for every one was looking at him. The King began:

M

'Now let us see how many crimes you have committed. You have broken your oath—isn't that right?'

'Oh! quite correct, your Majesty.'

'And you have rebelled against my daughter?'

'Quite correct, your Majesty.'

'And ,you have intended to murder her?'

'Just so, your Majesty.'

'And you tried to marry her?'

'I should have been only too pleased, your Majesty.'

'And you don't repent, do you?'

'Not at all, your Majesty.'

'And the right punishment for each of your crimes is death?'

'Just so, your Majesty.'

'But I don't care to sentence you to death—it's not hard enough. I sentence you to live underground for ten thousand years.'

'Ten thousand years, your Majesty!'

'You can go at once, and if I catch

you above ground—I shouldn't like to be you.'

'No, your Majesty. Good-day.'

And he kissed his hand to the Princess, and bowed gallantly to the Prince of India, and then the ground gave way under him—and he has never been heard of since. But the King turned to the Prince of India and said :

'You may go now, Prince.'

The Prince looked astonished.

'I do not quite understand, your Majesty,' he said.

The King looked at him and said :

'You seem to be uncommonly hard of understanding, cousin of India. I said, You can go.'

'But I don't want to go, your Majesty,' the Prince answered, getting a little red.

'Oh, don't you?' said the King; 'from what I heard of a certain pleasant conversation in a certain summer-house you seemed to have important affairs of State that demanded instant attention.'

Here the doctor suddenly remarked :

'If you will excuse me, your Majesty, I beg to differ from you when you refer to that conversation as pleasant. I myself heard it, or rather overheard it, and all I can say is I thought it most unpleasant,—most. That is, if your Majesty will excuse my remark.'

'But I won't,' said the King suddenly. 'I believe it was you that suggested I should be confined to a dark cellar for three weeks without food—eh !'

But the doctor suddenly remembered that he had an important case that demanded instant attention.

The King turned to the Princess and said :

'Well—I suppose you can settle it for yourselves, you two, because I'm going now.   I shall come and see you every seven years.   Good-bye.'

And he suddenly turned into the Brown Owl, and flitted noiselessly off, before they could say 'Good-bye,' or anything else.

The Prince found that he could manage to postpone his affairs of State indefinitely, and in a few days the Prince and Princess were married and lived happily ever afterwards.

THE END

www.ingramcontent.com/pod-product-compliance
Lightning Source LLC
Chambersburg PA
CBHW020229030726
47497CB00009B/3005